KANDEE'S CRUSH

An Unforgettable Tale of Being Caught in the Middle

Tamia Gore-Felton

Copyright © 2016 Tamia Gore-Felton.

All rights reserved. No part of this book may be reproduced, stored, or transmitted by any means—whether auditory, graphic, mechanical, or electronic—without written permission of both publisher and author, except in the case of brief excerpts used in critical articles and reviews. Unauthorized reproduction of any part of this work is illegal and is punishable by law.

ISBN: 978-1-4834-4438-3 (sc)
ISBN: 978-1-4834-4437-6 (e)

Because of the dynamic nature of the Internet, any web addresses or links contained in this book may have changed since publication and may no longer be valid. The views expressed in this work are solely those of the author and do not necessarily reflect the views of the publisher, and the publisher hereby disclaims any responsibility for them.

Any people depicted in stock imagery provided by Thinkstock are models, and such images are being used for illustrative purposes only. Certain stock imagery © Thinkstock.

Lulu Publishing Services rev. date: 02/09/2016

Dedicated to my ultimate crushes:

Eula M. Holmes
Ruby M. Meyers
Nathaniel A. Gore
Semoward Meyers
Yvonne (Smoochie) Smith
Allen D. Smith
Erin D. Jacobs
I'll love you all forever and ever.

Prologue

Valentine's Day: February 14, 2010

"Kandee, you have an important phone call." Echoed the restaurant owner over the PA system. As I dried my hands on my apron, I hurried to the phone. "Hello, Head Chef Camden speaking," I answered. "Is this Kandee Camden, Jacob Camden's wife?" The voice asked curiously. "Yes, this is she. Is everything alright?" "No, everything isn't alright, your husband and I have been in a relationship for the past two years, and I'm pregnant."

Just that fast I felt like I had to throw up and shit, all at the same damn time. The aroma from the different types of food cooking made me feel worse by the second. "Excuse me?" I asked, as the other cooks in the kitchen talked and carried on like they were on the hit television show, *Top Chef*. The voice on the other end of the line then repeated everything that was said the first time. I was sure that I heard her correctly. However, I just had to make sure before I got an attitude. "Well, that's nice to know, being that it's Valentine's Day and everything," I sarcastically replied. "I just wanted to let you know because I'm tired of sharing Jacob. I'm ready to have him all to myself, and he was taking entirely too long to tell you."

"Who did you say this was again?" I asked as I wiped my face with the bottom of my apron. "Um, I didn't say." "Oh, so you can call my job and tell me about my husband; but you can't tell me who the hell this is? You're nothing but a coward; until you're ready to tell me who this is, stop calling my damn job and worrying me about my husband." As I was about to hang up, the voice on the line cleared its throat. "This is Erica." "Erica, did your mother give you a last name? Or is it just Erica Homewrecker?" I asked, with an attitude.

"The name is Erica Sumpter, soon to be Erica Camden" she boldly answered. "Alright Mrs. soon to be Camden, you've got two minutes to spill your guts." With that said, Erica spilled the beans. She and Jacob had been intimate countless times, the two had met at the post office, shockingly she had one abortion, and she knew how the inside of my house looked. The heffa even knew about my oldest son contracting an STD from his cheating girlfriend.

I wanted to reach my hand through the phone and yank her tattle tell tongue out. As she kept talking, I listened and watched the second hand on the clock reach the twelve and told her that her time had expired. "I hope you got everything out, now do yourself a favor and don't call my job ever again or else I will call the police and tell them that you are harassing me," I said before I slammed the phone down and went to the ladies room.

After talking to the woman on the phone who seemed to know just as much as I did about my life, I played out different scenarios of how Jacob would react to the news after I confronted him. I saw Jacob on his knees begging me for another chance, I saw him showering me with gifts, and even sending dozens of vases of flowers to my job. As the scenarios became a familiar blur in my mind, my emotions got the best of me, and I started to shake. I wasn't sure if I could keep a straight face while I felt so crappy on the inside. I hated to leave the restaurant right now because it was Valentine's Day and we were swamped with couples.

I counted to one hundred, took a deep breath, and gathered myself before leaving the ladies room. I headed back to the salmon that I had previously taken out of the refrigerator and chopped the head off. At the moment, I wished I could do the same thing to my no good, sorry excuse for a husband. All I ever got out of this marriage other than stretch marks and constant pain in my ass were my two handsome sons; Jr and Ty. Sometimes I wish that I could turn back the hands of time and wake up in my pastel pink room, filled with floral patterns and teddy bears. Thinking about my past had truly gotten me through tonight's busy Valentines rush.

By the time the end of the night came, I'd sautéed over three hundred scallops and filled over one hundred soup bowls with my famous corn chowder. When I wasn't thinking about the good old days, my mind was filled with questions. When, why, and how did this keep happening to me? Question marks swirled around in my head along with the name Erica Sumpter. Why couldn't my husband keep his man parts to himself? I knew that I was a good wife. I'd never cheated on Jacob and had been nothing but sincere to him since the day we said our vows.

To be honest, I knew something was going on with Jacob. He had changed, and I overlooked it, I thought it was because he was about to turn forty. But now I realized that the new cologne and workout routine was all because of an affair. All the problems that I'd been having out of my husband made me want to go back and relive my entire childhood. Yeah, it was rough, but at least, I would get to feel my mother's arms wrapped around me and get a sweet kiss from my first crush Levi.

After the staff had cleaned the kitchen, it was immaculate, the stainless steel gleamed as I locked the back door behind the last crew member. I was supposed to be out in the parking lot with them now. Letting my car warm up and finding something to listen to on the radio, but not tonight. Instead of going home to my cheating husband, I was going to make myself at home in my office. I figured I would teach Jacob a lesson and not come home tonight.

After I had set the alarm, I grabbed a bottle of wine out of the refrigerator and went into my office. Just as I turned on the radio, Lloyd whispered "I Want You" I wanted him too; hell, I wanted anyone who would treat me right. After I had drunk half of the bottle of wine, I relaxed a little and took off my shoes. After calling Trudy twice, I realized that she was either sleep or getting busy with her tall, dark, and handsome boy toy. When I looked at the clock, I saw that it was a little after one in the morning and decided that I would call her back in thirty minutes or so.

As the thoughts went around inside of my head like a merry-go-round; the mischief that Trudy and I used to get into when we were younger made me smile. I laughed as my eyelids got heavy, subconsciously I put my head down on my desk. Then I heard Levi's voice telling me how pretty I was, as I slipped back into time.

1

In the beginning: November 1990

I hummed along to the radio that always played in the kitchen as I cooked. My body moved back and forth to the catchy tune while I iced a lemon pound cake. The pots on the stove bubbled and spit steam as the timer started buzzing on the counter top. The turkey was ready, and I couldn't wait to see how it looked. After baking it all night, I was finally about to pull the big bird out of the oven.

While peeking through the little glass window on the oven door, I saw my mother entering the kitchen. After yawning, she put on an apron and said, "Happy Thanksgiving my love." "Happy Thanksgiving Mom," I replied, as I put on the old burgundy oven mitts and opened the oven door. "It sure smells good in here Kandee, I bet no one is going to believe that you made this year's Thanksgiving dinner by yourself, I can't even believe it." Mom said as she placed a cooling rack on the counter.

After carefully pulling the tray out of the oven a bit, I grabbed the handles on the side of the pan and lifted it up. When I set the pan on the cooling rack, I let out an enormous sigh of relief. The hard part of my dinner was over. Mom checked out the turkey and delightfully said, "Kandee, this turkey looks better than mine did last year. I can't wait for your grandmother to see this; she's going to swear that she taught you everything you know about cooking. Get the Polaroid honey, I want to take a picture of this."

While she snapped a photo of the golden bird, she continued to talk about my cooking. I giggled to myself, I could hear my grandmother saying "Kandee, this is a beautiful meal. Everything tastes so lovely." Grandma always described things as lovely and beautiful. I thought it was the cutest thing ever. The words lovely and beautiful floated around in my head as I stirred the butter beans and checked on the chicken bog. With the macaroni and corn bread now in the oven, I boiled some water to make tea.

A few minutes later, mom complained about a headache. "Maybe you're just hungry," I said while I cut some lemons up and measured sugar for the tea I was about to prepare. By the time the tea was ready, mom had the whole turkey, sliced and on a platter. "I wish my head would stop hurting like this, maybe I should eat a piece of this turkey." "Go ahead eat some, I'm dying to know how it tastes," I replied with a grin. When she put a piece of the turkey in her mouth, she chewed for a bit in silence.

"Come on mom, how does it taste?" I whined as I stomped my feet. "Darling, it's absolutely delicious. To be only fourteen years old, you can give any woman in this family a run for their money when it comes to cooking. Kandee, you definitely have a gift." "Aww, mom do you really mean that?" I asked, as I snatched the other piece of turkey out of her hand and ate it. "You little brat," she shouted, as she chased me around the kitchen.

***

As our family members started to arrive, I was in hog heaven. I didn't know if I was more excited for everyone to know that I cooked the entire meal or if I was happy to see some of my cousins that I hadn't seen since last Thanksgiving. While the adults gathered in the living room, the children sat outside on our wrap around porch. We played a game called "That's my car." The rules of the game were simple, you watched the street for a passing car, and if you liked the car, you yelled out "That's my car."

While we played the game, everyone chatted and got reacquainted as we waited for more guest to arrive.

"That's my car" I yelled, as soon as I saw a green Mercedes driving towards our house. Some of my cousins high-fived me, but others were mad because they didn't claim the car first. I paid them no attention as they yelled things like, "you cheated" and "that's not fair" as the car pulled into our yard. All the kids on the porch watched in silence as the car came to a stop and the engine turned off. We all wondered who was behind the dark tinted windows, as all four doors on the Mercedes opened simultaneously.

It was my Aunt Joyce and her children; Larry, Rich, and Trudy. When I saw Trudy, my heart skipped a beat. Trudy was my favorite person in the world other than my grandmother and my mom. She was two years older than me, I looked up to her and considered her to be the sister I never had. As everyone ran off of the porch to greet them, I made a beeline for Trudy. After we hugged, I noticed that Trudy was wearing makeup. Not a lot, but more than my mom would ever let me wear. I hugged Aunt Joyce, Larry, and Rich, after all the other kids mauled them.

As everyone made their way back to the porch, Trudy and I stood beside the car and caught up. "Trudy, your mom's car is fly, I know this had to cost a lot of money," I said, as I put my face up to the window and looked inside. "This isn't my mom's car; it's her stupid boyfriend's. He told her that she could drive it today if she sucked his thing when we get back home" Trudy said. "What? Eww, that is so gross! How do you know that?" I replied. "I heard them talking. As soon as they go into mom's room and shut the door, I go into the bathroom and put my ear up to the wall to see what they are talking about."

"I hear a lot of things that go on in that bedroom," Trudy said, as she smiled at me and pulled me towards the porch. Even though I was curious to find out what else Trudy heard, I didn't ask any further questions because I knew that eavesdropping wasn't polite. Whenever we sat down on the porch swing, I changed the subject. "Guess what," I said, in a whisper. "What?" Blurted Trudy, with wide eyes. "I cooked all the food for Thanksgiving. Mom is going to make the announcement before we say the grace." "I'm so proud of you, I can't wait to eat. Mom didn't make breakfast this morning. She said that we didn't need anything to eat because it may ruin our appetites for Thanksgiving dinner." "I only had a piece of turkey this morning," I added, as my stomach growled.

"So, how is Aunt Rita doing? I know she had her first round of radiation this week. I heard mom say that…" Trudy immediately stopped talking when she noticed the look of horror on my face. "Kandee, I'm sorry, you didn't know did you?" Before I got too emotional, Trudy took my hand and walked me to the edge of the yard. Tears slid off of my face and onto the sidewalk, as I tried to catch my breath. Trudy asked me if I wanted to hear more and I shook my head yes. She talked until we approached the stop sign at the end of the street and I stopped walking.

I felt like I was having an outer body experience as Trudy told me about the tumor in my mother's brain. "I'm sure Aunt Rita will be okay Kandee, please don't worry," she said, as we made our way back to my front yard. "That's my car" yelled the kids on the porch, as they claimed a rusty hoopty that sputtered along the street. As they pointed and laughed, Trudy and I bypassed them and made our way into the house.

When we reached the upstairs bathroom, Trudy sat on the side of the tub as I washed the tear stains off of my face. "I wish they would have told us. What kind of parents keeps a secret like this away from their kids?" I asked, as I shook my head and thought about my two younger brothers, Samuel, and Rickey. Trudy then replied, "The kind of parents that don't want you to worry, I guess. Kandee, you know that worrying never helps anything, and I'm sure Aunt Rita and Uncle Jack will tell you guys at the right time" Before I could say anything else, I heard the dinner bell ring.

The dinner bell was a tradition at all of our family gatherings. When everyone heard it, we knew that it was time to drop whatever it was that you were doing and make your way to the dining area. As Trudy and I made our way downstairs, we saw all the younger children walking in a single line. It looked like they were at a school heading to lunch. As I cut through their perfect line, I headed towards mom.

When the dinner bell rang again, there was complete silence. Everyone knew that it was time to say the grace. Before mom gave the rundown of the menu, she made the announcement I had been waiting for all day. After she had cleared her throat, she said, "I'm happy to see all of you, and I'm grateful that the good Lord allowed us to be here today. I want everyone to know that my dear Kandee prepared the dinner we are about to eat. She stayed up most of the night chopping vegetables, baking cakes, and prepping food for today's dinner. Before we say our grace, let's give my baby a round of applause to show her how much we appreciate her cooking for us today."

After the round of applause, my grandmother blessed the food. Then the children formed another line and waited outside of the bathroom to wash their grimy little hands. While most of the women started fixing the children's plates, they shouted out praises to me. I smiled, as I heard one of them say, "Only fourteen years old and she made the entire Thanksgiving dinner, she is going to be a chef one day, just wait and see."

I blushed at all the attention that I was receiving, as I filled a few cups with ice. Then my attention fell on my mother. She laughed and talked with her aunts and cousin. As I poured sweet lemon tea into the red plastic cups, I wondered if her head was still bothering her and if she felt like entertaining all of these people in our home today. Those two questions were bothering me, but what I wanted to know most of all, is when our parents were going to tell my brothers and me about her sickness.

***

After everyone was done eating, the children went back outside after mom gave them a box of sidewalk chalk. As they filed out in a single file line, mom yelled, "Draw something pretty, maybe it will bring the property value up." We all burst out laughing. My mom said some of the craziest things. While the women cleaned up after dinner, most of the men gathered around our floor model television in the den. They hooted and hollered about the football game they were watching. The rest of the men were on the porch smoking cigars, pipes, or cigarettes. That was a nasty habit that most of the men in our family had. If I ever got a husband, he definitely wouldn't be a smoker.

I gave my mother a hug while she was in the middle of putting away the dishes. "Mom, mingle with the other women, Trudy and I will finish cleaning the kitchen." I whispered. She kissed me on the cheek and told the other ladies to stop cleaning. I knew that they wanted to relax, gossip, and brag in private. As the older ladies left the kitchen, they told my mother how sweet I was. I looked at Trudy and with a blank face, then I finished putting the dishes up. We worked silently in the kitchen until I turned on the radio. When I heard Lisa Stansfield's, *All Around the World*, I sang along. Trudy joined in with me as we filled the Tupperware with what was left of Thanksgiving dinner. While we sang I noticed how beautiful Trudy's voice was; I never knew she could sing.

The last thing we did in the kitchen was wiped the counters off and sweep the floor. We were going to mop, but we decided that it wouldn't be a good idea since so many people were still in the house. God knows, we didn't want anyone to slip and fall. Before we left the kitchen, I unplugged the radio and tucked it under my arm. Trudy and I were going to continue this party in my bedroom.

As we entered my room, I closed the door behind us. I then plugged the radio into the socket and turned it on. While Trudy looked around my room, she touched my posters that were hanging on the walls and even sat at my homework desk. After she had looked through the drawers, she said, "You got your period yet Kandee?" "No" I mumbled softly. "Well, you better be glad because that shit hurts like hell. I got my period last year; the only good thing about having your period is that you start to develop boobs, I went up a full cup size. This boy at school always wants to carry my books and sits with me on the bus. They weren't paying me any attention until I got these beauties" Trudy said, with a giggle as she shimmied her shoulders from side to side.

"Trudy, you are something else," I said, as she continued to wiggle like a worm in hot ashes. "I will get my period when it's time. Besides, I'm not worried about having boobs at the moment all I want is for my mom to be okay." Trudy then replied, "I'm sure Aunt Rita will be fine, she is a strong woman. Do me a favor, try not to worry, and don't let anyone know that your mom is sick because if you do, I'm going to be in big trouble."

The both of us laughed as Trudy sat down on the bed beside me. "Kandee, you are so lucky to have your room, I hate sharing a room with my brothers. They always leave their funky underwear all over the place. One time they put a pair of stinky socks inside my pillowcase and I slept on that funky pillow for two whole nights before I realized those socks were in there" She said, as she laid back on my bed. "Well, Samuel and Rickey don't even come in my room. They just stand at the door and talk to me. They say it's too many shades of pink and teddy bears in my room for them to come in here."

Trudy and I didn't get to talk much longer after that because Larry barged into my room and said, "Trudy, get your big butt downstairs, mom said it's time to go." Trudy and I both looked at Larry and yelled, "Get out!" He still stood there until Trudy picked up one of my church shoes and threw it at him. When he finally left, Trudy and I shared a hug. After Trudy put on her shoes, she walked over to my desk and wrote her address down. She then pulled one of my desk drawers open and retrieved a clear thumb tack and stuck the paper on the wall.

As soon as we walked out of my bedroom, Aunt Joyce yelled Trudy's name from the bottom of the stairs. When she saw us coming, she said, "Didn't your brother tell you that we were about to leave?" Trudy looked at me and said, "No ma'am." With Larry in Aunt Joyce's reach, she smacked him in the back of the head. Trudy and I tried our best to hold in our laughs while Larry rubbed his head and attempted to tell Aunt Joyce the truth.

When we got downstairs, I noticed that everyone had left except for grandma and grandpa. Aunt Joyce fussed at Larry and Rich as we walked outside. The boys were almost ready to fight over the passenger seat. After everyone had hugged and wished Aunt Joyce safe travels, Trudy gave me another hug and whispered: "Remember, don't tell anybody." I shook my head okay, as Larry got slapped in the back of the head again. When they finally pulled out of the yard, we waved and laughed about Larry and Rich, fighting over the front seat.

After we got back into the house dad shut the door, and we all sat in the living room. We all talked about how good Thanksgiving dinner turned out. When my little brothers asked for cake, mom went into the kitchen and fixed everyone a slice. When I went to help her, I saw her leaning on the counter with her head in her hands. "Mom are you alright?" I asked as I wrapped my arm around her shoulder. I must have startled her because she jumped and immediately reached for some napkins that were on the counter. "I'm not feeling too good baby. Can you do me a favor? Please fix everyone some cake and ice cream? I'm going to take a shower and lay down."

"Sure mom" I replied after I gave her a warm hug and told her that I loved her. After I had fixed the ice cream and cake, I pulled dad to the side and told him that mom wasn't feeling well. Dad nodded his head and headed back into the living room to entertain grandma and grandpa. I lost my appetite and threw my cake and ice cream in the trash before I headed upstairs.

After I checked on mom, I took a shower and sat down at the foot of my bed. I felt really down, even though everyone went back for second helpings during dinner today. I couldn't stop thinking about mom and her sickness. That's when the tears began making their way down my face, and I slid down onto my knees. I stayed on my knees praying for a long time. When I finally got in bed, I thought about Trudy and how she eavesdropped on her mom and found out all kinds of things. While I drifted off, I thought that I should start eavesdropping too.

2

Facing Reality

That night I woke up to the sound of an ambulance siren. As I jumped out of bed, my heart dropped down to my toes. When I opened the door to my bedroom, I saw my brothers hugging my grandmother in the hallway. All of them were crying, I knew this couldn't be good. "Grandma, what's going on?" I yelled. Grandma only looked at me and said, "Honey, it's your mother, she stopped breathing in her sleep and…" That was all that grandma could get out before I ran towards mom and dad's room. Just as I was about to go in, the paramedics rushed pass me with my mother secured to an ambulance cart.

As they quickly and carefully maneuvered the cart down the stairs, I got a glimpse of my mother's face, and she looked like she was sleeping. I yelled "Mom, are you okay? Mom, can you hear me? MOMMMMM!!!" I collapsed into a ball of nothing outside of my parent's bedroom door, and my dad rushed to my side. Wearing only pajama bottoms and a sweater, he held me in his arms for a second and whispered that everything was going to be alright. He then ran down the stairs, and I gathered myself and ran after him. As I tried to get into the back of the ambulance with dad. My grandpa grabbed my arm and pulled me back.

When the ambulance drove away, I stood in the street and cried until I could no longer see the flashing lights. My Grandpa held me in his arms until I was ready to go back into the house. For the rest of the night, I was a nervous wreck. Even after dad called from the hospital and said that mom was in stable condition and resting. After everyone had found out that mom was alright, they went back to bed. When I got in bed, I couldn't sleep at all. I stared at the ceiling until my eyes crossed and I fell into a deep sleep.

The next morning grandma cooked a big breakfast. Samuel and Rickey ate like they had not eaten in days. I, on the other hand, messed over my food and only took one sip of the fresh squeezed orange juice that grandma made. My stomach was in knots. I wanted to ask grandma and grandpa about mom's sickness, but I also wanted to keep my promise to Trudy. I told her that I wouldn't say anything. Aunt Joyce would skin her alive if she found out that Trudy had been eavesdropping.

With Trudy on my mind, I decided to write her a letter. Before I could get up and empty my plate into the trash can, Samuel asked, "Can I have your bacon and toast?" I slid my plate over towards him and headed to my bedroom. After walking over to my desk, I snatched the paper that Trudy wrote her address on, off of the wall. After reading the address, I realized that she didn't live far, only the next town over. I needed to talk to her after what happened last night. I needed to know if she had been eavesdropping and found out any new information about my mom.

I don't recall Trudy ever saying what Aunt Joyce's boyfriend's name was. All I knew is that he had a beautiful green Mercedes. As I thought about ways to get in touch with Trudy, other than writing her a letter, I decided to call my friend Denise from school. When she answered, I heard her mom say, "Don't be on that phone long you little heffa, I'm expecting a phone call."

After we had talked for a few minutes, I cut to the chase. "Do you have any relatives that live in Florence?" "Yeah, I have a few cousins and an uncle. Why, what's going on in Florence?" Denise asked, "I have a cousin named Trudy that lives there, and I need to talk to her, but I don't know the phone number, all I have is her address." "Well, what's the address?" She asked, as I looked at the paper and read it to her. "My cousin lives on the same street, I'm sure she can tell your cousin to call you." "Really

Denise, thank you so much, remember to give your cousin my phone number and tell her that it's very important." "Alright, I will do it as soon as I get off of the phone," she said, as we both hung up.

Not even ten minutes later the phone rang. I crossed my fingers as I picked the telephone up and said hello. "Kandee, are you okay? I've been thinking about you all night. I heard what happened to Aunt Rita" Trudy said. "I think so, Trudy have you heard anything else about my mom's condition? Everyone around here has their lips buttoned" I said. Trudy took a deep breath and said, "I know everything, but I don't want to tell you. Please don't make me."

"It's bad. Isn't it?" I asked. "Yeah, it's bad" answered Trudy. "How about you call me back tonight, your dad is supposed to be talking to you and your brothers today" Trudy suggested. I could feel the saliva in my throat get thick as I answered Trudy by saying "Okay." Before Trudy and I ended the call she gave me her phone number and told me that she loved me. After I hung up, I just sat there. I couldn't move because the thought of growing up without my mother had me paralyzed with fear.

***

By the time daddy got home, I had cried over a gallon of tears and my pillowcase was soaked. As I heard daddy's footsteps getting closer to my room, I turned my face towards the wall. I didn't want him to know that I had been crying. When he entered my bedroom, the door creaked. "Kandee, baby are you sleep?" He asked as he shook my shoulder softly. I didn't move; I wasn't ready to face reality. After he realized that I was asleep, he sat down at the foot of my bed and started to cry. Hearing such a strong man cry like that, made my stomach hurt.

As I turned over, I said, "Daddy, is mom going to be okay?" When he turned to see that I was awake, he sucked his tears up and said, I need you to come downstairs now. I need to talk to you and your brothers. When he left my room, he went to the bathroom across the hall. As soon as he shut the door, I got up and put my ear against it. For a second there was pure silence, and then I heard it; a deep sob that sounded like a dog that had been hit by a car.

I didn't know what to do, so I ran downstairs to get grandpa. When grandpa and I were on our way back up the stairs, dad met us halfway. "Son, please tell us what's going on," Grandpa said, as he held onto the banister. "Let's go into the den, get mom and the boys too" he insisted, as he took a deep breath.

After I had pulled grandma away from her crossword puzzle and the boys from in front of the television, dad and grandpa were already sitting on the couch in the den. Samuel fussed about not being able to finish watching *Bill Nye: The Science Guy* and dad shushed him as soon as his butt hit the couch. There was total silence until grandma walked in with her robe on and a mug filled with coffee.

Dad then cleared his throat as he began to speak. I called this family meeting to tell you that Rita is sick. "We know that daddy, we saw her leave in the ambulance last night. She's coming back home today. Right Daddy?" said Rickey. When dad dropped his head, I knew what was coming next. "Your mom isn't coming back home. She has to stay in the hospital because she has a sickness in her brain. Kids, I need for you to get dressed, so you can go and see your mother" Dad announced. Grandma put her coffee mug down and went to sit beside dad. As she rubbed his back, his eyes turned into faucets.

"Daddy, why are you crying? What kind of sickness does she have in her brain? Can the doctors fix it?" Asked Samuel. While dad wiped his tears away with the sleeve of his shirt, he said, "I'm sorry son, but it can't be fixed. We need to go and tell your mother good-bye." "What do you mean Dad? Tell her good-bye. Where is she going?" Shouted Rickey. Before dad could say anything else, I jumped up and yelled, "Rickey and Samuel, stop asking all of those damn questions. Mom is dying, that's what you're telling us right Daddy. Our precious mother is about to be funeralized and buried deep under the cold, damp earth in a box."

Everyone stared at me as I realized what I just said. The whole sentence that I just blurted out was supposed to stay inside of my head and not come out. I couldn't believe that I just cussed in front of my dad, grandma, and grandpa. I'd never been disrespectful to them. Feeling overwhelmed I busted out in tears and apologized. When dad stood up, I thought he was going to take his belt off and beat me, but he didn't. He took me in his arms and held me tight. As we released tears, the rest of the family got up and formed a circle. We all cried and rocked back and forth as grandma said a prayer for the entire family.

***

On the car ride to the hospital, no one said a word. Dad drove, and grandpa sat in the front with him. As the silver Suburban made stops and turns through the city, I felt car sick, and wanted to throw up. I was anxious about seeing mom in the hospital bed. When I looked at my brothers and grandma, they were all cuddled up on one another. The boys were leaning on each other, and my grandma had her frail arm stretched around both of them.

When we pulled into the hospital parking lot and parked. Dad turned off the engine. No one said a word, all you could hear was seat belts unbuckling, heavy breathing, and doors closing. As we walked into the hospital, we all followed dad like the kids did on Thanksgiving. We stayed in a straight line until we got on the elevator. The soft music that played as we made our way up to the third floor didn't relax me at all.

As we poured out of the elevator, other people went inside and tapped their feet to the soft music. When the elevator door shut, I realized that I was the only one left standing there. The rest of my family was gone. As I walked down the only hall that lead to the elevators, I figured that it wouldn't be hard for me to find my family. When the hall split and I didn't know which way to go, I was just about to ask for help, until I saw my grandmother in the distance. She was standing outside of a hospital room.

I wanted to yell "Grandma", but there were posters that read "Shh, people resting" and "Please be quiet." My heart thumped louder as I walked towards her. When I got close enough, I whispered, "Grandma, I thought I was lost until..." That's all that I could get out before my father opened the door of the hospital room. "Kandee, come with me darling," he said, as he took my hand. I saw fresh tears on his face and saw my brothers in the corner clinging to my grandpa.

Next, my eyes fell upon my mother. As dad held my hand, he led me closer and closer to the hospital bed. The only sounds that were present was a continuous beep from one of the machines that my mom was hooked up to and my two brothers sobbing. "Mom," I said, as I reached and touched her warm hand. "She can't hear you Kandee; she just took her last breath a few moments before you came in," Dad said as he pulled me closer.

"Last breath. No, mommy isn't dead. She just can't be." I yelled, as my legs grew weak. If my dad hadn't been holding me so tightly, I would've fallen on the hard hospital floor. As dad maneuvered my limp body to a nearby chair, my stomach felt queasy. When grandma heard all the commotion in the room, she came in to see what was going on. I totally lost it and sobbed until I felt like I had to vomit.

"Kandee, you need to calm down, you can't make yourself sick," She said as she pulled paper towels out of a silver box that was directly above the sink. After wetting the towels, grandma knelt down in front of me and wiped my face. With a damp face and a mind full of denial, I looked at my mom's body in the hospital bed. Although I knew she wasn't breathing, it sure looked like she was.

***

The Funeral was on a Thursday, and the church was packed. Mom's funeral service only lasted for an hour, but it was a lot of tambourine playing and shouting. I can honestly say that it wasn't a sad funeral, and I barely cried at all. Everyone held up good until it was time for the casket to be rolled out for the final viewing. As the flower girls and Pallbearers marched out of the church, I sat patiently until it was time for the family to stand up.

After the funeral director had given us the go ahead, our entire family stood up. The old pews at the church squeaked and creaked as the first row made our way down the middle of the church. I glimpsed some of my mother's coworkers and people from the community with their heads down as we walked by. As we moved closer to the foot of the glossy casket, my eyes teared up. I saw my mother laying there with her hair curled so pretty. Seeing her hair like that reminded me of the wedding picture in the frame back at home.

I tried not to look at her face, but I couldn't resist. I couldn't take my eyes away from her. I stood at the casket for almost a full minute before I moved a muscle. I would always remember how my mother looked in that casket for as long as I lived. When my feet finally did move, I realized that dad had his strong arms around me. As he guided me to the church grounds, we both were startled by a loud scream. When I turned around, Aunt Joyce was on the floor in the church foyer.

Larry, Trudy, and Rich look terrified when they saw their mother sprawled out on the floor of the church. Dad left my side immediately and sprinted back into the church foyer to check on his sister-in-law. I watched from a distance until other family members started to gather around. I squeezed through the crowd to see Aunt Joyce laying there, as still as can be. After dad had kneeled down beside her, he yelled, "Someone wet this at the water fountain," as he waved his dry handkerchief in the air.

By the time one of my cousins returned with the handkerchief, Aunt Joyce was becoming conscious. Dad delicately placed the handkerchief on her forehead; her eyes fluttered then she focused on him only. When she realized who he was, she smiled and reached out for him. As the onlookers watched dad help Aunt Joyce to her feet, I wondered if they saw what I saw. There was a spark between them. Dad looked at Aunt Joyce like he used to look at mom a long time ago, back when they were madly in love. I had a feeling that something was going on between them, but I had to make sure I was right before I let Trudy know about it.

After Aunt Joyce was up off of the floor and back to her usual self, she went back to mom's casket and kissed her on the cheek. Then she walked away with tears falling from her eyes and got into the green Mercedes that she had driven to our house on Thanksgiving. I stood on the side of the church and watched Aunt Joyce until people spilled out onto the church parking lot. I could barely see anything now, thanks to the tall men and the ladies who wore the big fancy hats. I swear one lady wore a hat that resembled a fruit bowl on the top of her head.

When I saw Dad approach Aunt Joyce's car door; I maneuvered through the crowd, only to get stopped by random people who told me how sweet my mother was. When I finally could see dad and Aunt Joyce, they both were standing beside the Mercedes. As they talked, I focused in on their mouths. After trying to read their lips for a few moments, I realized that it wasn't going to work. So I did the next best thing, I focused on their body language and facial expressions.

I watched the two of them like a hawk until Trudy walked up and gave me a hug. "Why are you over here by yourself?" "I'm ready to go; I don't want to see them. I mean I don't want to see the funeral crew lower mom's casket into the earth. All I want to do is go home and be alone in my room." I replied. Trudy then linked her arm inside of mine, and we looked inside of the church foyer as the funeral workers closed the casket for the last time.

It hurt me to see them close the lid, but I knew there was absolutely nothing I could do about it. As I leaned on Trudy's shoulder, I saw my brothers with their arms wrapped around dad's waist. They buried their faces in his coat jacket while my eyes scanned the crowd for Aunt Joyce. When the pallbearers surrounded mom's casket and picked it up, I felt like my stomach was about to get upset.

As my stomach flipped and flopped, I walked over to my dad and said, "My stomach feels queasy, I'm going to the bathroom. I don't think I will be back in time to sit under the tent by the gravesite (which was only a few yards away) with the rest of the family." Dad looked concerned but nodded his head alright because he had his hands full with my brothers.

I immediately went back inside the church to use the bathroom, and Trudy followed close behind me. When I reached the small bathroom, I ran inside of the last stall and locked the door. I struggled with my dress and stockings and then my stomach made a tremendous rumbling sound. As bad as I wanted to line the toilet seat with tissue, I couldn't. My choice was either sit on the naked toilet seat with no barrier from the germs or just stand there and shit on myself. Those were my only two options, so I sat down on the cold toilet seat, and my bowels instantly released their contents.

Trudy said, "Damn, what did you eat, you're rotten. I'll wait for you outside in the hallway." "Okay," I answered, as I sat on the toilet. I waited for another ten minutes or so before I cleaned myself up. Trudy was right, I did stink. After I pulled and tugged on my stockings, they still sagged down between my thighs. I think grandma purchased the wrong size. I was so sick of playing tug of war with the stockings that I took them off and threw them in the toilet without thinking. When I tried to flush the toilet, nothing happened, and I instantly panicked and called for Trudy.

After trying to flush the toilet, again and again, we both saw the sign on the door of the stall that read "DO NOT USE-OUT OF ORDER." I was so embarrassed but thank God for Trudy's quick thinking. She looked under the bathroom sink and found a can of air freshener, a bottle of Lysol, and a plunger. While Trudy sprayed the room, I tried to open the bathroom window so that some fresh air could come in. It was useless; the window was painted shut. After wasting time messing with the window, I pumped the plunger up and down in the toilet and tried flushing it again.

"Trudy, it's not working" I cried, as I gave up. She didn't say anything. "Trudy," I whispered, as I peeked out into the hallway. "I'm coming," she said, as she entered the stinky bathroom with a pitcher of water from the church kitchen. When Trudy walked into the stall, she gagged at the mess I had made. Then she poured the water into the toilet. We both held our breath and crossed our fingers that the mess would go down, and it did.

I breathed a huge sigh of relief after I cleaned up the mess I had made. While Trudy waited for me to finish, she sat on the counter beside the sink. When I was done cleaning, I washed my hands and laughed as Trudy put the pitcher under the cabinet with the rest of the cleaning supplies.

As we were leaving the bathroom, a lady with a big hat walked by us and went into the stall with the sign on the door. I started to warn her about the sign but decided not to as Trudy and I walked towards the chatter in the church dining hall.

After looking around for a second, I saw the table where my dad and brothers were sitting. Grandma, Grandpa, Aunt Joyce, and her boys were seated at the table as well. Aunt Joyce sat beside dad, and I didn't like it. I wanted to ask her could I sit beside him, but I didn't want to make a scene. As Trudy and I sat down in the only two seats left at the table, a lady bought us each a drink and a plate filled with food. While we ate, everyone mingled and even asked for refills from the ladies who were doing the serving. I tried not to let Trudy know that I was watching Dad and Aunt Joyce, but she knew something was up because I ignored her and stared in their direction.

3

Sneaky Snake

That night Grandma, Grandpa, and Trudy stayed over. Trudy, Grandma, my brothers, and I were gathered in the kitchen eating a smorgasbord of things that family and friends had bought over after the funeral. It was pretty quiet in the house until the phone rang. Grandma answered the phone and handed it to Trudy who was sitting down. "Hey Ma," Trudy said, as she tilted her head and held the phone with her shoulder. While Trudy talked to her mother, I finished up my glass of juice and started washing the dishes. Just as I wondered what Aunt Joyce wanted, Trudy said, "Okay mom, hold on." Then she yelled, "Uncle Jack, mom needs to talk to you, pick up the other phone."

I turned my head and looked at Trudy as she held onto the phone until dad yelled from upstairs "I got it, Trudy, hang up the phone." As Trudy hung up the phone, I wondered what Aunt Joyce and Dad could be talking about. That's when the thought entered my mind to eavesdrop. Before I walked out of the kitchen, I switched the radio on low and crept into the living room. I was startled by a nasty belch Samuel let out from the kitchen, but that didn't deter my plans of eavesdropping.

My heart beat faster, as I sat down on the couch and slowly picked up the receiver. I held my breath as I heard Aunt Joyce say, "Jack, you looked so handsome in that suit today, I wanted to rip it off of you." Dad then responded, "Thanks, maybe I can wear the suit again, so you can do just that." I listened for another minute or so before I quietly put the phone back on the hook. I automatically wanted to run upstairs and give dad a kick in the nuts, but most of all I wanted to find Aunt Joyce and snatch her bald.

As I placed the receiver back on the hook, I heard dad open the door to his bedroom and come down the stairs. I quickly went back to the sink in the kitchen before he reached the living room. When he entered the kitchen, he asked, "Was someone on the phone, just now?" Grandma replied, "Not that I know of, we all were in the kitchen." I could have kissed grandma; she was so into her crossword puzzle and a slice of strawberry cheesecake that she hadn't even noticed that I left the room. Trudy noticed, though.

After the kitchen was clean, dad checked the front and back doors to make sure they were locked. While he made sure the house was secure, I turned off all the lights except for the one over the kitchen stove. With everyone else already upstairs, dad and I headed upstairs too. From out of nowhere, he asked, "Can I talk to you in my room for a minute?" I instantly felt nervous, but I didn't let him know that. I calmly answered, "Sure, let me check and see if the boys are really showering or just standing outside of the shower while the water runs." Dad chuckled, as I took a few more steps and knocked on the bathroom door. "Who is it yelled Rickey?" "It's me, you better be in that shower washing and not in there messing around. I'm going to check behind your ears after you're finished."

Rickey grumbled under his breath as I peeked inside the bathroom. Steam escaped past me, as the smell of *Lever 2000* flew up my nostrils. He was really in the shower; I couldn't believe it. All of his clothes were scattered on the white tile of the bathroom floor. After I quietly closed the door, I went to see what Trudy was doing. I watched her from the door of my bedroom as she bopped around with headphones on her ears and a Walkman attached to the waist of her pajamas. I wondered if she was listening to my Janet Jackson cassette before I walked towards my parent's room.

Before entering the bedroom with dad, I took a deep breath. "What's up?" I asked as I sat on the old trunk at the foot of the bed. "I just wanted you to know that I am proud of you, you held up great at the funeral today, pumpkin." "Thanks," I said, as I got up to leave the room. "Wait a minute. I'm not finished yet" he said before he continued talking. "Kandee, I'm going to need your help with the boys now that your mother is gone. I'm certain that you can help me keep them in line. Do you think that you could help me do that?" "Yes, sir. I can do that" I answered, as I started to tear up.

As he continued to talk, I noticed the smell of the bedroom. The whole thing smelled like my mother. Even though she wasn't here, her scent was everywhere. I tried to focus on what he was saying, but there was no use. I was mesmerized by the aroma. While his lips moved, I got up and walked over to the dresser. All of her perfume was there, lined up in a row. Without thinking, I picked up her favorite fragrance, *Elizabeth Arden's Red Door*. I slowly removed the cap, took a whiff, and almost melted. "Dad, can I have this?" I belted out, interrupting whatever it was that he was saying. "Uhh, yeah baby. Sure, you can have any of your mother's belongings. Whatever you want is yours."

I then rubbed my eyes and hoped that the tears would go away, but they didn't. As I stood in front of the dresser, my heart began to feel so heavy, and I didn't feel like being in the room with dad. All I wanted to do was to hug my mom. Her scent was overpowering, and I had to get out of this room before I got sick again. On top of that, the thoughts of dad messing around with Aunt Joyce had returned. "Dad, I'm not feeling well. Can we talk about this tomorrow?" I asked as I walked towards the bedroom door. "Sure" he agreed, as he nodded his head.

Back in my bedroom, Trudy was making a pallet on the floor. She had six blankets piled up, like the mattresses in the children's book *The Princess and the Pea*. "You better take your bath or shower now because your brother has an upset stomach and he said that he was about to drop a bomb" Trudy warned, as she took one of the pillows off of my bed.

Without saying a word, I immediately went to my drawer to get my night clothes.

After gathering all of my things, I quickly made my way to the bathroom in the hallway; only to find out that I was too late. Samuel was already in there, and the stench that came out of the bathroom was horrible. I was going to beat on the door and tell him to hurry up, but the thought of taking a shower in a bathroom that smelled like *Lever 2000* and hot shit wasn't on my agenda for the night. Since there were no other bathrooms in the house, I was forced to ask dad if I could take a bath in his room.

When I entered dad's room, I held my breath for a second because I didn't want to smell my mother's scent. Dad had no problem with me using his bathroom after I told him about Rickey stinking up the entire hallway. After I had shut the bathroom door, I inserted the stopper in the drain of the tub and turned the faucets on. While the water ran, steam filled the bathroom, and I undressed. Just as I put one foot into the tub, the phone rang, and I heard him answer "Hello."

I quickly removed my foot from the bath and walked to the bathroom door to see if I could hear anything. What I heard made me wish that I would have toughed it out and took a bath in the funky bathroom down the hallway. I overheard him talking in a whisper, "Baby, I know. Maybe we can meet up tomorrow; we can get it on in the back of the Suburban like we did last week. I made sure all of that junk was cleaned out of there so nothing would be in our way."

At that moment, I regretted listening in on his conversation. My face felt like it was about to slide off and my stomach started cramping up. As I quietly walked away from the door, I could hear dad chuckling. I wanted to listen some more, but my stomach was upset again. When I sat on the cold toilet seat, goosebumps appeared on my arms and legs. My head swirled around and around, as I wondered if he was talking to Aunt Joyce.

After I had taken my bath, I cleaned out the tub and opened the bathroom door. Dad was still on the phone. When he saw me, he talked in a more serious tone and even said some things about work. "Good night Daddy, love you," I said, as loud as I could. Hoping that whoever he was talking to heard me. After removing the phone from his ear, he replied, "Good night, love you too pumpkin."

As much as I hated to go to the hall bathroom, I had to put my dirty clothes in the hamper. To my surprise, it didn't smell that bad. After brushing my teeth and putting my night bonnet on, I went to my bedroom. Trudy was trying to get comfortable on her pallet of blankets when I walked in and closed the door.

"Trudy, we need to talk," I said, as I flopped down on my bed. "Yes, we sure do. Aren't you supposed to give up your bed to me, since I'm a guest?" She asked, with a smirk on her face. "Don't even try it, Trudy, you know I don't give up my bed to anyone." "Well, can I at least, have another pillow?" She asked, as she walked over and snatched a pillow from under my head. She laughed, as she sat down beside me on the bed, but I didn't because I was about to tell Trudy about Dad and Aunt Joyce.

"Now that you have your extra pillow. I'm going to ask you something, but promise that you won't be mad at me for speculating." Trudy looked at me with wide eyes and said, "If this about your Uncle Jack and my mom, yes they are screwing. They've been screwing around for the longest." My mouth fell open, as my heart skipped a beat. "Trudy, why didn't you tell me?" I yelled, as I punched her in the arm. "Ouch! I didn't want to let you know because I didn't want to get into the middle of it. Your mom knew about it" confessed Trudy, as she rubbed her arm.

"Trudy, I heard Aunt Joyce on the phone with dad tonight. I was eavesdropping. Do you remember when he came into the kitchen earlier and asked if anyone on the phone?" "Yeah," she said. "Well, I was listening, and I heard Aunt Joyce say that she couldn't wait to get dad out of the suit he was wearing today" I replied. "Honey, I heard more than that when I pressed my ear up against the bathroom wall at our old place. Mom and Uncle Jack have the most intimate conversations. I heard him tell her that he loved her one night, after they…" Trudy had confessed before I cut her off.

"Stop it, Trudy! I don't want to hear any more of this; I just can't take it" I cried. Then I lay down and released tears into the sleeves of my polka dot pajamas. Trudy tried to sooth me by rubbing my back, as the tears continued to flow. I was hurt; I thought that dad loved mom. How could he do her this way and how could mom let dad dog her out like that? There had to be more to this Dad and Aunt Joyce situation, and I knew Trudy knew everything, but I was afraid to ask.

After Trudy had made sure I was okay, she got another pajama top out of my drawer, and I changed. As I took the tear stained pajama top to the hamper in the hallway bathroom, I heard dad's baritone voice behind his closed bedroom door. I looked back to see if the door to the boy's room was closed and it was. Then I crept closer and closer to dad's room door. I knew that I was probably going to regret it, but I put my ear against the door. I heard him say, "We can make this work baby, it's only a matter of time." I swallowed hard, as I continued to listen and my stomach began to hurt.

When I went back into my bedroom, Trudy was on the pallet fast asleep. I was going to wake her up and tell her what I had just heard, but I didn't. Instead, I pulled the covers back and got in the bed. While I listened to her snore, I replayed the entire funeral inside of my head. When I got to the part of seeing my mom for the last time, I started crying. I couldn't believe that she would never grace us with her presence again. I continued to cry until; I heard a soft knock on my bedroom door. "Who is it?" I asked as I wiped the snot and tears away with my hand. Rickey answered, "It's me, and I can't sleep. Can I sleep with you tonight?" "Sure," I said, as I tossed a pillow at him and pointed towards the foot of my bed.

As soon as Rickey got situated at the foot of the bed he started talking. "Did you see Aunt Joyce fall out at the funeral today? I thought that she died too." "Yeah, that was crazy" I replied. From there we talked about the entire funeral, mom's casket, flowers, and the food at the repass. When I told him what happened to me in the bathroom, he burst out laughing. I was so glad that Rickey came into my room. I needed him tonight, as much as he needed me.

***

Kandee's Crush

The next morning dad made breakfast, but it didn't taste good. There were egg shells in the eggs, the grits were scorched, and the toast was burnt. I tried to eat, but Trudy, Samuel, and Rickey gave me the evil eye. One of them kept kicking me under the table until I asked dad if I could cook something else. At first, I thought that he was mad until he said, "I was wondering how much of these crunchy eggs I was going to have to eat before you said anything." We all laughed as he collected all of our paper plates and tossed them in the trash.

I whipped up the meal in no time, and we all were smacking our lips and pouring lots of maple syrup onto our French toast. After we had finished eating Dad, Rickey, and Samuel cleaned up the kitchen, while Trudy and I relaxed in front of the television. "Girl, Uncle Jack made some nasty ass eggs. I'm so glad that you rescued us with those fabulous omelets." After her confession, I elbowed Trudy in her side and said, "You know you can't whisper, you better stop cussing before he hears you."

As soon as I got the words out of my mouth, daddy walked into the den and thanked me for making breakfast. My heart dropped because I thought he was coming to fuss at Trudy for using bad language. When he sat down on the striped couch right across from Trudy and I, beads of sweat formed on my forehead. I had a guilty conscience and felt like he knew that I'd been eavesdropping on him. My stomach churned, as the three of us sat and watched reruns of *Bewitched*.

When Rickey and Samuel joined us in the den, I felt better. The two of them lay on the floor and tried to wiggle their noses like the lady did on television. After *Bewitched* had gone off, I opened the doors on the coffee table and pulled out all of the photo albums that were inside. Everyone got an album and joked about different things as they flipped through the worn pages. I laughed and joked too until I saw a picture of Aunt Joyce sitting on dad's lap. They had to be teenagers, maybe 17 or 18 years old. When I got Trudy's attention, I pointed to the picture, and she looked surprised. I started to say something to dad, but he was consumed with the burgundy photo album he was looking through. Plus, I didn't want to mention anything about this in front of the boys.

For the rest of the afternoon it drizzled and the boys were bored out of their minds. Since they couldn't go outside, they pestered us to play a game with them. After asking Trudy and I to play *Trouble* over twenty times, we finally gave in. As Rickey set the game up, dad came from upstairs with his truck keys jingling in his hand. "I'll be back in a few hours, keep the door locked and no company," he said, as he shut the entry door.

Even though dad left, his cologne lingered in the den. When Samuel got a whiff of the strong smelling fragrance, he sneezed. "Dad sure has a lot of cologne on" he complained, as he sneezed again. Just as he made the complaint, I looked at Trudy, and she already knew what I was thinking. After letting the boys win the game. Trudy and I headed upstairs.

The door creaked as Trudy and I entered the room. The smell of his cologne was still present in the air and made my nose burn. After covering my nose with my shirt, I went into the bathroom. The smell of shaving cream mixed with cologne almost made me throw up. Droplets of water ran down the side of the shower, and the bathroom mirror had steam on it. I knew that this meant dad had just taken a shower; I wondered where he was going, as I checked the trash can to find a box of black hair dye. Since dad had a bald head, I assumed that the dye was for his facial hair.

When I was done snooping in the bathroom, I joined Trudy back in the room. After looking through the drawer on dad's side of the bed, she found a piece of paper with a name scribbled on it. Whoever wrote the name had terrible handwriting. I think the name on the paper was Rochelle and on the back of the card was a set of lips prints, made with the reddest lipstick I had ever seen. I wondered who this Rochelle lady could be as we put everything back the way it was when we entered the room.

As soon as we closed the room door, Rickey and Samuel were coming up the stairs. Trudy and I quickly pretended that we were on our way back downstairs, as we met them on the staircase. "Wanna play *Old Maid?*" Asked Samuel. "Nah, we're gonna watch MTV until daddy comes back," I said, as we made our way back to the den.

After Trudy had turned on the television, we both got comfortable on the couches. She was on one striped couch, and I was on the other. I

Kandee's Crush

heard the boys upstairs fussing about somebody cheating, and I thought to myself, "Dad's the cheater." As I nodded my head to the music that played, my eyelids got heavier and heavier. Before I knew it, I was awakened by a loud pop of thunder. As I rubbed my eyes, I tried to look at the clock, but I couldn't see it. I knew it was late because there was no light coming from the windows.

When I sat up on the couch, I put my feet on the floor only to step on Rickey. He moved a little but didn't wake up. I made my way to the window and looked outside to see that dad's truck wasn't outside. I wondered if he was with Aunt Joyce or Rochelle. After looking at the clock and seeing that it was only 9:30. I decided to call Aunt Joyce. When her boyfriend answered the phone, I knew that he wasn't at her house, so I just hung up. After trying to remember the number that was on the paper, I couldn't. I had to go back to dad's room and look inside the drawer to see what the number was.

I climbed the stairs in total darkness and turned on the hall light, as I reached the top of the stairs. Then I slipped inside of dad's room and went to the drawer on the side of the bed. Luckily, he left the lamp on, so I could see what I was doing. I searched for the number, but I couldn't find the paper. I could have sworn that Trudy had put it back in the drawer. As I looked around, I spotted a torn piece of white paper on the floor by the bed. I grabbed the paper and read the number. Just as I picked up the phone to dial the number, I heard the front door open. I put the phone down and heard heavy feet coming up the stairs and then I heard my dad cough.

I didn't know what to do and froze up for a second before I quickly put the paper back in the drawer and fell to my knees. I rolled under the bed just in time to see my dad's boots as he entered the room. As he sat on the bed, he kicked his shoes off and picked up the phone. After he had dialed a number, I heard a female voice answer, and then my dad said, "Baby, I made it home." The voice on the other end of the line replied, "That's good, I was worried about your drive home. It was raining really hard." He then responded with a chuckle, "We only live fifteen minutes away from each other. What do you think is going to happen to me that fast?" The lady on the phone said, "I don't know, I don't want anything to happen to you, I don't think I could live without your good loving."

I took shallow breaths while I heard my father and his lover talk about everything they did tonight during the thunderstorm. Dad laughed, as the woman on the other end of the phone, pumped his head up. "I didn't know you could last that long Jack; you really outdid yourself this time." "Well, I do what I can, sweet cheeks," he bragged, as he got comfortable on the bed. As much as I didn't want to hear them finish their conversation, I had too. If I moved a muscle, my cover would be blown.

Almost an hour later, he told his sweetie goodnight, and he even kissed her through the phone. After he had hung up, he went into his bathroom and started the shower. As soon as I heard him pull the shower curtain back and start humming, I rolled from under the bed and quietly exited his room. After I had entered my room, I got into bed and stared at the ceiling. I couldn't wait until Trudy woke up so I could tell her about this.

4

Seeing Red

After being out of school for a whole week, I was ready to get back into the swing of things. Now that Grandma, Grandpa, and Trudy had gone back home, and it was just Dad, Samuel, Rickey and I. That Monday morning I woke up an hour earlier than usual. The first thing I did was pull out all the stick pins in my mother's pin cushion and scattered them around on the thick carpet in the back of the Suburban. I made this booby trap for dad and whoever he was going to be frolicking around with back there. I laughed to myself, as I quietly shut the double doors to the back of the Suburban.

As soon as I got back in the house I heard dad's alarm going off. When I looked up the dark staircase, I saw the reflection of the boy's room light on the wall. That meant they were up; I knew they would be dressed and ready to eat soon. So, I cracked eight eggs and put on a pot of water for the grits. When the smell of breakfast made its way up the stairs, I heard feet hustling down the staircase. As the rumbling got closer, I poured apple juice into four cups and set them beside the place settings on the table.

I'd fixed everyone's plate and joined them at the table, just in time for the grace. "God is great, God is good, let us thank him, for our food, Amen." That was Rickey and Samuel's favorite prayer because it was the quickest. Those jokers were always ready to dig into a plate of hot food. Over breakfast dad asked us how we slept. I replied, "I slept well."

Samuel said, "I had a dream about Mom, it was a good dream though", and Rickey only replied, "Good" since he was too busy shoveling food into his mouth.

When we all were finished eating, I quickly washed the dishes and put them in the pale yellow dish drain to dry. I then made dad's lunch and went upstairs to get ready for school. I wore a pair of stonewashed *Jordache* jeans with a purple v- neck top. After I had tied up the purple, teal, and white shoe strings on my *LA Gear* sneakers, I went into the bathroom and curled my hair the best I could. I did a pretty good job, thanks to Trudy giving me a tutorial before she left yesterday.

After I unplugged the curlers, I went into my room, tossed my backpack over my shoulder, and went downstairs. The boys were on the couch watching cartoons but quickly switched the television off when they saw me heading towards it. "Come on knuckleheads, it's time for us to walk to the bus stop," I said, as I checked the entry door to make sure it was locked.

As dad backed up out of the driveway, he smiled and waved, as he drove away in the long Suburban. While he smiled and waved good-bye; I thought "I bet you won't be smiling when you get stuck with those stick pins, you sneaky bastard." I continued to watch the Suburban until it turned the corner. "There's the bus," said Rickey, as Samuel moped closer to the curve. After watching Rickey and Samuel get on the elementary school bus, I adored the purple polish that Trudy polished my nails with yesterday. While I patiently waited for the high school bus, a few kids from the neighborhood walked up.

They all said good morning as they chatted among themselves. "Sorry to hear about your mom." One girl said as she adjusted the straps on her backpack. I only nodded and gave her a slight smile. I would have said something in return, but I didn't know how to respond to her. Should I have said, "Thanks" or "It's okay." I didn't know, so I kept my lips buttoned. I didn't want things to be more awkward than they already were. I was cool with everyone at the bus stop, and I could tell that they were uncomfortable and didn't want to laugh or show any signs of happiness around me; considering that my mother just passed away.

Kandee's Crush

I heard the brakes of bus 73 squeal before it even got to our bus stop. Everyone got in line as the bus turned the corner and came to a complete stop in front of me. I hadn't ridden the bus in a week, so the bus driver nodded his head as soon as he saw me. As I walked down the aisle to my assigned seat, I noticed that a boy was sitting in my spot. After looking at him like he was crazy, I boldly said, "You're in my seat." "No," I'm in our seat, he replied, as he pointed at the index card that was held up by gray masking tape. "Oh okay," I mumbled, as he slid over by the window.

For the rest of the bus ride, I kept quiet. We were only allowed to talk to the person to the left and the right of us. Since I didn't know the stranger in my seat, I looked up at his name again and read it. The tag read Kandee Blue and Levi Morrison. As Levi looked out the window, I checked him out. He was a cutie, but I think he had an attitude because he had to sit by the window. I would have sat by the window, but it was too late now. The bus was moving, and if either one of us stood up, we would get in big trouble with the bus driver.

As the bus driver stopped at stop lights, turned corners, and dodge potholes. I admired Levi. He had a creamy complexion with curly brown hair that was cut into a box shape. He also wore a thin gold chain around his neck. As bad as I wanted to say something to him, I couldn't. The cat definitely had my tongue. I didn't want to say the wrong thing, so I sat quietly until the bus came to a complete stop in the school parking lot. When the bus driver opened the door, all the kids stood up, except for me.

I waited until the aisle was clear, and then I stood up and got off of the bus. As I stepped up on the curve, I looked around to see where Levi had gone. I saw him walking with a group of guys that were on their way to the cafeteria. I wanted to follow him, but I had to go straight to my homeroom teacher and catch up on my makeup work before the bell rang.

I saw my friend Denise just as I walked into the hallway. She wore her hair in two long French braids and had on a black pair of oversized overalls. She gave me a big hug and caught me up on all the gossip. There was a food fight, a fist fight, and a stink bomb incident that she mentioned. I laughed, as we knelt down by our lockers and struggled with our combination locks. I had this combination lock since middle school, and I still had trouble remembering the code.

After Denise and I split ways, I went to my homeroom and greeted the teacher. Mrs. Warren gave me a side hug and asked me how I was doing. After chatting with her for a few minutes, she gave me all of my makeup work and I looked through it. I didn't have much to do; I probably could do all of the worksheets at lunch if the students didn't get too loud in the cafeteria.

When the bell sounded, I was already in my seat working on the morning work. When the other students started pouring into the classroom. I kept my head down and paid them no attention. When I heard a voice say, "Pass this to Levi," I looked up. Levi was in my class, and his seat was right behind mine. I couldn't believe it. I felt like God was doing me a favor for not eavesdropping on dad last night.

I turned all the way around, as I watched a girl pass Levi a note. I instantly got jealous, as he smiled and saw that he had dimples. When I turned back around in my seat, I thought of a way to get Levi to notice me. "Maybe if I wore a low cut shirt or some tight jeans tomorrow, he might pay more attention to me," I said to myself. In the mid-thought, the bell rang, and Mrs. Warren shut the door to the outside world. We were now in the land of English 9. When Mrs. Warren slapped her yard stick against the desk, everybody got quiet. They knew that she meant business.

After the announcements, Mrs. Warren gave us our assignment and paired us up into groups of two. I crossed my fingers, eyes, and toes that I would be able to work with Levi, but lady luck wasn't on my side this time. I had to work with the girl who wanted the note passed to Levi. All she talked about was Levi. How fine he was, how she loved his curly hair, how she loved his dimples, and the light brown color of his eyes. When I asked her if she figured out the answer to number three yet, she asked, "Do you think we would have cute kids together?" "What?" I squealed, in a high-pitched voice, as I scrunched my face up. "Not us, silly. I'm talking about Levi and I" she beamed.

This little heffa was getting on my last nerve, and I was just about to tell her when the fire alarm sounded. The class lined up while Mrs. Warren got her purse out of the file cabinet and told us to zip our lips. On our way out of the building, I saw Levi walking at the end of the line with some guys. I looked around and tried to find my aggravating partner, but she was nowhere in sight. I wondered where she went, as I kept up with the rest of the class.

When we saw a steady stream of smoke coming from one of the science labs, everyone picked up the pace and high tailed it onto the school lawn. As the fire truck pulled up, I saw my partner coming out of a smoky exit. When she reached Mrs. Warren, she was out of breath and gasping for air. "Where were you?" Mrs. Warren asked. "I went back to get my pocketbook," my partner said, as she sat down on the damp grass.

We had to stay outside for two hours. When we finally made our way back inside the school, it was time to go to our 2nd-period class. As everyone slid their chairs and desk back into the straight rows, Mrs. Warren wrote our homework assignment on the board. I quickly jotted the assignment down, as Levi walked by me. That was the last time I saw him until it was time to get on the bus that afternoon.

On the bus, I sat by the window this time. As Levi talked to the boy to the right of him, I started on my homework because I knew that I had to cook dinner when I got home. After Levi's friend got off of the bus, he got quiet and pulled the letter from this morning out of his pocket. When he unfolded it, my heart rate increased. As I pretended to do my homework, my eyes darted back and forth between my work and his letter.

Dear Levi,

> I know that you only been at this school for a week, but I am really digging you. When I first saw you last week, I knew that we were meant to be together. Every time I see you my heart skips a beat. Please say that you will be mine. I would love it if you would carry my books to class and eat lunch with me. Call me tonight, my

number is 555-9561. I'll be waiting for your call. I can't talk on the phone after 9. Please call before then. XOXO

Love Renee,

"Are you finished reading my letter?" He asked, as he shook his head and folded the paper up. I was beyond embarrassed and wished that I could disappear. "I'm so sorry" I mumbled, as he started laughing. "It's all good Kandee Blue, where were you last week? I had the whole seat to myself." I put my head down and told him why I was out of school. "I'm so sorry to hear that. Do you mind if I ask you what happened?" Honestly, I did mind, but I wanted to talk to him, so I told him about my mother's headaches and tumor.

Before I knew it, I knew his story. He moved here with his father because he got a great job offer with the city. His mother wasn't in the picture at all anymore, she was a junkie and stayed behind in Georgia. She chose the streets, drugs, and alcohol over her family. When Levi talked about her, I could tell that he hated her. After he had said that he lived on the next street over, I got all warm on the inside. I couldn't believe that he lived so close to me.

As we continued to talk, the girls on the bus looked our way and gave us long stares. I knew that they were jealous of me because I got to sit with Levi. When it was time for him to get off of the bus, he stood up and said, "See you in the morning." "Okay," I said, as I noticed the folded note in the seat. "Levi you forgot your letter" I yelled, as he walked closer to the front of the bus. "Call her and tell her that I'm not interested," he said, with a smile.

Before I stuffed the note in my backpack, I watched Levi pull his key out of his pocket and walk up the sidewalk to his house. It wasn't anything spectacular, just a brick house with white shutters and a little bit of grass. As the bus pulled away, I was on cloud nine. I slid over to the spot where he had been sitting, and it was still warm.

The cloud nine feeling didn't last long because the bus driver stopped me as I was about to get off of the bus. "Kandee, if you ever yell on this bus like that again, I will write you up and have you suspended off the bus. You got that?" He barked, as he pointed his finger at me. "Yes. I understand," I replied, as I stepped off of the bus. The rest of the kids laughed at me until the bus driver turned around and yelled at them too. The last thing I wanted to do was get kicked off of the bus. I needed to get my dose of Levi every day.

As soon as I got in the house I checked on Rickey and Samuel. They both were sitting in front of the television watching Reading Rainbow. While the show had their attention, I retrieved the note out of my Purple JanSport backpack. I unfolded the letter and looked at the phone number, then I picked up the phone and started dialing. I could tell that my partner answered the phone; her voice was so babyish. After she answered the phone, I let her have it. "Renee, this is Kandee. I was calling to tell you that Levi said he wasn't interested in being your boyfriend. He also doesn't want you to write him any more letters."

Levi didn't say that he wanted Renee to stop writing him letters, but at that moment, I knew that he wanted me to tell her that. There was a short moment of silence before Renee said anything else and I wasn't sure if she heard me or not. So I told her again.

What I wasn't expecting was for Renee to start crying. I didn't know what to say, so I only said, "Don't cry, there are more guys you can pass notes to." After Renee had stopped crying, she agreed with me. Since I was curious about why Renee went back inside the school to get her pocketbook during the fire drill, I asked her. "What was so important in that pocketbook that you risked your life for?" Renee replied, "If you must know, that is a three hundred dollar purse and I had my expensive makeup inside, I couldn't just let it burn up." Even though I didn't understand how a pocketbook and some makeup could make one risk their life, I replied, "Oh, okay."

After I hung up the phone with Renee, I washed my hands and started chopping sausage links, bell peppers, mushrooms, and onions. I decided to make a quick spaghetti dinner with garlic bread and corn on the cob. By the time dad got home, the house was filled with the aroma of an Italian restaurant. While the boys finished up their homework and dad took a shower; I took the trash out. As I walked by the back of the Suburban, I looked in to see if the stick pins were visible. I couldn't see a thing because of the tint on the windows. After I put the bag of garbage in the can, I opened one of the doors to the back of the truck and rubbed my open palm across the carpet. When I got stuck by a pin, I knew that dad behaved himself today or, at least, didn't have sex in the back of the truck.

***

The rest of the week flew by, and it was already Friday. I thought about mom a lot this week. I missed everything about her. Taking on her role of cooking and cleaning was already getting to me. That morning when the alarm went off, I didn't feel like moving at all. My stomach was hurting really bad; I never felt this kind of pain before. As I lay in bed, my stomach cramped more and more. I knew that I was lactose intolerant and that I shouldn't have had that ice cream last night after dinner.

Before I walked into the bathroom, I knocked on Samuel and Rickey's bedroom door. "Wake up guys," I said, as I reached the entry to the bathroom. After I shut and locked the door, I pulled down my pajamas bottoms and sat on the toilet. My eyeballs almost popped out of my head when I saw blood on the seat of my panties. I now knew why my stomach was hurting, and it wasn't because of the ice cream I'd eaten. I had started my period. I wasn't totally clueless about having a period; Mom and Trudy told me a little about it. I knew that I needed to shower, find some maxi pads, and I needed to tell dad.

I panicked I pulled up my underwear and pajama bottoms, I then walked down the hall to dad's bedroom door and knocked on it. He didn't answer, so I turned the knob slowly and called out to him. As I entered the room, I saw that his bed was made up, like he never even slept in it at all. I flicked on the light switch and looked in the direction of the bathroom; he wasn't in there either. I wondered where he was and went into his bathroom to help myself to the remainder of mom's maxi pads. There were two packs of them on the shelf where the washcloths and towels were. Before I left the bathroom, I looked in the medicine cabinet and found a bottle of Advil. After reading the back of the bottle, I poured two of the pills in my hand and left his room.

I knew that I wasn't going to be able to cook a big breakfast this morning, I was already fifteen minutes behind schedule, and I still had to take a shower. After I had closed the door to the bedroom, I heard him talking downstairs. I wondered who he was on the phone with this time of the morning. As much as I wanted to go back into his room and pick up the phone to eavesdrop, I didn't. I had to get myself together because I had to look good for Levi.

After swallowing the Advil with a handful of water at the sink, I took a shower. I then dressed in black jeans and an oversized white RUN DMC t-shirt. When I put on my black and white *Fila's*, I curled my shoulder length hair and went downstairs to the kitchen. Rickey and Samuel were dressed and watching television; dad was still on the phone in his work clothes from yesterday. When he saw me, he said, "Don't make me any lunch today, I'm not going to work." I uttered, "Okay", as I walked through the den. The wheels inside of my head were turning, as I cracked some eggs and grabbed a loaf of bread. "Joyce you know that you don't have to put up with that" I heard dad say. I wondered what happened to Aunt Joyce; I couldn't wait to call Trudy when I got home after school today.

The toast popped up out of the toaster, and I put the butter and jelly in the middle of the table. When I called the boys to come and eat, they ran into the kitchen like two little ponies. They looked at me like I was crazy when they didn't see any meat or grits on their plates. Before they had a chance to say anything, I said, "Do you see what time it is? We only have six minutes to eat." When the boys looked at the clock, their eyes got big, and they gobbled up their food.

On the way out of the house, I made Rickey put cocoa butter on his face and elbows because he was beyond ashy. Dad removed the phone from his ear and gave each of us a hug before we marched out of the front door. As soon as we walked to the curve, the elementary school bus was there waiting for them. We got out of the house just in time. When the boys were on the bus, I walked down a little further to my bus stop.

As the other girls came to the bus stop, they ignored me and talked about how fine Levi was. I was mad now, but they were going to be so jealous when I got on the bus and sat down beside him. When the bus pulled up, I was the first one in line to get on. As I climbed the stairs, I saw Levi slide over in our seat, and a big grin spread across my face. "Good morning Kandee," he said, as I flopped down beside him. "Good morning" I replied, as I looked to see the girls from the bus stop trying to get a glimpse of Levi.

After we greeted each other, we talked about what we did yesterday after we got off of the bus. Levi said that he partially cleaned his room up and ate a nasty frozen dinner. I told him that I washed two loads of clothes, helped my brothers with their homework, and cooked meatloaf, homemade mashed potatoes, and sweet peas. I could tell that Levi's mouth was watering after he said that meatloaf was his favorite.

"So what did you eat for breakfast?" I asked as I heard his stomach growl. "Nothing, I usually eat at school because I'd rather sleep an extra 10 or 15 minutes. Plus I can't cook, I would probably burn down the house" he replied. I listened carefully to everything he said, as we carried on our conversation until the bus pulled into the parking lot at school.

When we got off of the bus, I saw Denise waiting for me at the corner of the building. I blushed, as I walked towards her. "What are you so happy about this morning?" She asked. "I think that I'm in love with Levi." Denise looked at me like I was crazy. "In love!" she repeated, as she held her trapper keeper close to her chest and giggled. "I see the way you look at him. You're not in love. What you have is a full blown crush" Denise squealed. I could only smile when she confirmed what I had known since the first day I saw him. I had a major crush on Levi and wanted to be his girlfriend.

5

People are Talking

For some reason, Denise didn't eat breakfast at home this morning. So instead of hanging out in the hallway until the bell rang, we went to the cafeteria. The cafeteria walls were huge panes of glass, and you could see what was going on in the inside from the outside. It had been a long time since I came into the cafeteria for breakfast. I always ate at home. Just from looking at the window, I saw that much hadn't changed. There were different cliques formed at every table. The preps all wore *Lee* jeans and *Keds*. The jocks wore school attire and school colors. The nerds didn't all wear glasses, but hung around a table piled high with books. The hippies wore colorful loose fitting clothes and smelled like marijuana. I was sure that I caught a contact high as Denise and I walked by them.

When we got into the line, I watched the lunch ladies scoop powered eggs, two sausage links, and a small biscuit onto colorful trays. Even though I wasn't hungry, I grabbed a tray and a juice box then gave my ticket to the lady at the register. While our eyes searched for a place to sit, I saw Levi. When he saw Denise and me, he motioned for us to come over. The guys that were sitting with him paid us no attention. Levi slid over, but there was just enough space for one person. When Denise told me to go ahead and sit down, I didn't hesitate.

I was so close to Levi that I could feel his body heat and smell his cologne. It only got better because Denise sat down on the remainder of the bench and pushed me even closer to Levi. I couldn't believe that we were this close. I didn't want to eat in front of him, so I offered him my tray, and he took everything but the juice. As he ate, I drank the juice and talked to Denise.

I watched the second hand on my watch until the bell rang. The students cleared the cafeteria quickly and headed to their classes. As I walked towards the exit, Levi yelled, "Wait up. We're going to the same place, so we might as well walk together." I thought I would melt; this was turning out to be an awesome day; minus the whole period thing.

When we got to class, we saw that Mrs. Warren wasn't here and that we had a substitute teacher. After the substitute had introduced himself; he handed out thick packets of work to everyone. As some students started to complain, the substitute said, "If you can keep it down, I will let you choose a partner to complete your classwork with." The next thing I heard was desk and chairs sliding around. I figured that no one wanted to work with me until Levi slid his desk beside mine.

Being that the packet was so thick, we didn't have time to talk about anything other than the work that was in front of us. Which was perfectly fine with me, just being close to Levi for ninety solid minutes had my mind blown. I was so consumed with being near him; I nearly forgot to go to the restroom to check my maxi pad. When the bell sounded, Levi slid his desk back behind me and reminded me to put my name on my paper before I handed it into the substitute.

For the rest of the day, I was beyond happy and couldn't wait to get on that long yellow bus. My period was now the last thing on my mind, and it was almost time for the end of the day announcements. As I waited patiently for the principal to stop talking on the intercom, I thought about Levi. He was fine, just like Renee said. His bright smile could light up a dark room. I secretly wondered what our kids would look like if we were to get married. I wanted to cook for him, I was going to see if I could make him; something special this weekend.

When the bell finally rang, I maneuvered my way through the hallway and sprinted to the bus parking lot. I chatted with Denise until I saw

Levi get on the bus. After telling Denise good-bye, I hustled to bus 73 as a line started to form in front of the bus doors. While the kids took their time boarding the bus, I wanted to yell "Get on the damn bus already", but I didn't want to make the bus driver angry.

Just as I made it up the steps of the bus, I saw Levi and he saw me. He smiled at me as I walked down the aisle. When I reached our shared seat, he said, "What took you so long? You usually beat me on the bus." I wanted to tell him that I was procrastinating because I wanted him to sit by the window. If he sat by the window, I would have him blocked in, and he wouldn't be able to talk to anyone. But instead of telling him the truth, I replied by saying, "Well, aren't you nosy."

After laughing, he said, "How about you let me sit on the outside today, I'm tired of being by this window." The smile on my face faded, as I said, "Oh, okay." When he stood up, I took my backpack off and squeezed by him. It looked like my plan had backfired and I was going to have to share Levi with one of his buddies that sat in the seat beside ours.

As everyone settled into their seats, the bus began to move. To my surprise, he hadn't said a word to his friend and focused all of his attention on me. I laughed, as Levi told me how he stole an extra slice of pizza today at lunch. He said that he stacked one piece on top of the other, and the lunch lady didn't even notice.

When it was time for him to get off the bus, he stood up and dug into his back pocket. After he took out two pieces of folded paper that looked a lot like notes, he handed them to me. "Don't open those now, wait until you get off of the bus" instructed Levi, as he strolled towards the front of the bus. About a half dozen girls, not including me watched as he got off of the bus. When the bus started to move again the same girls that admired Levi looked at me and rolled their eyes.

I'm usually laid back and don't let little things get to me, but before I knew it, I had rolled my eyes back in their direction. Maybe it was the PMS that made me so annoyed and short today; I thought as I unfolded one of the folded papers that Levi had given me. I know that he told me to wait until I got home, but I just couldn't. I had to see what the note said.

My eyes got wide as I opened the paper up. Levi had drawn a picture of me, and it was breathtakingly beautiful. He never told me that he had such talent. The picture looked just like me, my brown skin, shoulder length hair and even the small scar on my chin from a bike accident when I was younger. I hated that he had folded this picture; it should have been in a frame. I didn't know how I was going to get the creases out of the paper; maybe I could iron them out and find a frame to put it in.

Levi had mad skills. He could have drawn anything or anybody, but he chose to draw me. I felt so special, and I couldn't wait until Monday to tell him how much I loved it. I couldn't wait to tell Trudy and Denise about the picture too. I was new at this but, I guess this meant that Levi has a crush on me too.

I was startled when a voice yelled "Kandee Blue, are you getting off of the bus today?" When I looked up, everybody on the bus was looking at me. The bus driver laughed as he said, "This is your stop, and you better get off this bus before I take you back to school." "I'm sorry," I said, as I grabbed my things and bolted down the aisle. After the driver had closed the door, I heard the remainder of the kids laughing at me as the bus drove away. I knew that they weren't going to be laughing long because the bus driver was going to tell them to shut up.

When I started walking the other girls that rode the same bus as me didn't say anything. They usually said, "Have a good weekend" or "See you later" but today they said absolutely nothing. I knew they were jealous because they saw Levi hand me those notes. I debated on opening the other piece of folded paper until I heard Trudy yell my name and I looked up. She was waving at me while standing on the front porch.

As I walked past the hedges, I saw Aunt Joyce's beat up Toyota parked beside dad's Suburban. Both vehicles were filled to the rim with a variety of things, at a glance, I saw a lamp, bedding, and piles of clothes. I wondered what was going on, as Trudy went to her mom's car and grabbed an arm full of clothes. "Girl, you will never guess what happened," Trudy said, as she shut the car door with her hip. "What?" I asked as I helped her with the clothes in her arms.

"Mom and her boyfriend got into it yesterday real bad. I didn't even have to eavesdrop because they were talking so loud that I could hear them in the living room. It's a good thing the boys were outside playing or else they would have heard all of that cussing and fussing." "What were they cussing and fussing about?" I asked Trudy with a concerned look on my face. "About my mama cheating on him. Someone told mom's boyfriend that they saw his car parked at one of those cheap motels downtown, you know the one's where you pay for the room by the hour. Mom tried to deny it, but her boyfriend found a receipt from the hotel in her purse."

"Dang, so what are you guys going to do? Stay with us?" I asked as Trudy put the pile of clothes on the couch. "Yep, that's the plan. I know that people in the community are going to be talking about this. So get ready to be talked about at school, at church, and everywhere else" Trudy warned. "So where's everybody at?" I asked as I looked around. "They are in the basement, cleaning it up and trying to make it livable. I think it's possible, but it's very musty down there."

Even though I didn't like the idea of having Aunt Joyce living with us, I didn't want my family out on the streets. I didn't know how this was going to work, but I knew I didn't have much of a say-so because I was only a child. As I thought about the sleeping arrangements, I got a headache. I sure hoped that Aunt Joyce was going to sleep down in the basement. The guest room was super small and didn't even have a closet. With all of the clothes I saw in the back seat of the Toyota, I knew that Aunt Joyce had to have a closet.

***

After four hours of cleaning, rearranging, and bringing in items from out of the Suburban. Aunt Joyce and her bunch were all moved in. The basement was now a makeshift bedroom. It now contained two sets of bunk beds, several bean bags, a lumpy couch, and a floor model television. The boys were beyond excited about their new living quarters. Aunt Joyce got the boys room, and Trudy got the guest bedroom with no closet. She wasn't thrilled about that, but at least, she wasn't in the basement.

That night Aunt Joyce cooked liver and onions along with dry rice and string beans. It wasn't my favorite meal, but I ate like it was. I was happy that I didn't have to cook. The boys scarfed down their food and hurried back down to their dungeon of doom. I knew by tomorrow morning the basement would smell like fart, old gym socks, and armpits, but that wasn't my problem, I planned on never going down there again. As Trudy and I cleaned up the kitchen, Aunt Joyce and Dad finished helping the boys make their beds and hung all of their clothes up on a white plastic rod that ran from one side of the basement to the other.

After the boys were all settled in, I took a shower while Aunt Joyce and Trudy made themselves at home. I felt uneasy about Dad and Aunt Joyce's rooms being so close together, but there wasn't a thing I could do about it. When all of the lights were out, I walked down the hallway to Trudy's room and told her that I started my period. She wasn't surprised; she said that she knew that it would come sooner or later. "So did you tell your dad yet?" Trudy asked. "No, I'm kind of ashamed. I don't even know how to tell him."

"Well, maybe you should tell my mom. Do you think that you would be comfortable telling her?" Trudy asked. "I guess so," I said, as Trudy yelled for Aunt Joyce to come to her room. "What's the matter?" Aunt Joyce said as she came running into the room. I immediately noticed how skimpy her night clothes were, but I didn't say anything. "Mom, Kandee started her period." "When?" Asked Aunt Joyce. "Today," Trudy and I said, in unison. "Aww, why didn't you say something honey, I wouldn't have asked you to help lug all of that stuff down to the basement today if I would have known that. How are you feeling now darling?" She asked.

"I feel okay, my stomach was hurting this morning, but I took two Advil's, and I used some of mom's maxi pads" I replied. "Alright, it sounds like you know what you're supposed to do. Trudy, show Kandee how to keep up with her cycle on a calendar tomorrow" said Aunt Joyce. "Sure thing mom." After I had talked with Trudy for a few more minutes, I left her alone to get comfortable in her new room.

***

At 4:32 in the morning I woke up and remembered that I never opened the other folded paper that Levi had given me. After searching for it frantically, I remembered that I left my backpack downstairs. When I opened my room door, I heard snoring coming from Trudy's room. I crept quietly down the stairs and picked up my backpack from by the foot of the stairs. On the way back up I heard someone say, "Shh, you've got to be quiet or else you will wake the girls."

As I wondered what was going on, I put my ear to my dad's bedroom door and heard the bed squeaking. Then I heard soft moans. I prayed that he was watching porn or some late night television show as I went Aunt Joyce's room and quietly turned the door knob. When I looked in the room, all I saw was an empty bed. After I closed the door back quietly, I went back to my room and debated on waking Trudy up. I was about to go to her room until I heard dad's room door open.

I cracked my door to see Aunt Joyce tip-toeing from Dad's room with a sheet wrapped around her. A part of me wanted to open the door and bust them, but then another part of me couldn't get up the nerve. I decided I better leave my lamp off until in the morning and put Levi's note under my pillow. After tossing and turning, I fell asleep for what seemed like forever.

When I woke up, I smelled breakfast cooking. I wiped the crust from my eyes, got up and stretched. Right away I noticed that I messed up my sheets and pajamas. "Stupid PMS," I thought as my stomach griped. I quickly stripped the linen of my bed and took my clothes in the bathroom. I figured I could wash my linen and take a shower at the same time. I sat on the toilet until the washing machine started, and then I got in the shower. After I had lathered up, I remembered Levi's note. I quickly jumped out of the shower with water and suds dripping from my body and opened the lid to the washing machine.

I dug around in the warm water and prayed that the note was still intact and legible. When I saw little pieces of paper floating around in the wash, I knew that the agitator had probably destroyed it. Just as I started to give up, it surfaced. After I had it in my hands, I realized that it look like a cornflake that soaked in milk for way too long.

As I unfolded the wet paper, I wondered if this was another drawing or a letter. I got frustrated as the paper clung to my wet hands and ripped apart even more as I tried to be gentle with it. All I could make out were the smeared words that read "Dear Kandee" at the header of the paper. That's how I knew it was a letter while I looked at the rest of the paper that wasn't still floating around in the washing machine. I couldn't read the body of the letter because it looked like a sidewalk chalk hopscotch did after it rained on it. The color was still there, but you had no idea what it used to be.

While I stood stark naked in front of our evil washing machine, suds and water continued dripped from my body. I felt horrible, I couldn't believe that I had washed Levi's letter. On top of that, my cramps were getting worse by the minute, and I had just remembered that I had to tell Trudy about Dad and Aunt Joyce bumping and grinding last night.

After I had lost all hope of figuring out what the illegible letter read, I threw it in the trash can by the toilet. The way that this morning was going, I knew that the rest of my day was going to be shitty from this point forward. After I dried off, I peeked into the hallway to see if the coast was clear. When I saw that it was, I darted to the hall closet and grabbed some new linen for my bed and ran into my bedroom.

While I got dressed, I wondered what Levi had written in his letter. Maybe he asked me out or even included his phone number in the letter. I made my bed up and continued to think about the letter some more. Then I quickly ran back into the bathroom and got the letter out of the trash. On my way back to my bedroom, I passed by Trudy. She looked like she was an extra in the movie *Night of the Living Dead*. Her gown was twisted, and her hair was standing up all over her head. Aunt Joyce was going to get her for not wearing her night bonnet.

When I got to my bedroom, I lay the wet letter on my window sill and hoped that the sun would dry it and possibly make some of the words reappear. I knew I was hoping for too much, but you never know. Miracles did happen, but only on television. As I talked to myself inside of my head, Trudy interrupted me by saying "Good morning." "Yeah, whatever" I replied, as I rubbed lotion on my face.

"Well, what's got you upset already today?" Trudy asked. "First of all, I heard my dad and your mom having sex early this morning. I even saw Aunt Joyce hurry back to her room with a sheet wrapped around her naked body" I said, with an attitude as Trudy covered her mouth with her hands. "Let me finish before you say anything," I snapped, as Trudy shook her head. "After I eavesdropped on Dad and Aunt Joyce, I came back into my room. Only to remember that Levi, the guy that I want to marry one day and possibly have lots of kids with, had written me a letter, and I forgot to read it. Considering that Dad and Aunt Joyce had just finished doing their business, I figured one of them may pop in to check on me, so I put the letter under my pillow and decided that I would read it in the morning. Only when I woke up, I was a bloody mess and so were my sheets, so I stripped my bed and forgot that the letter was mixed in with the laundry. After I started the shower and washed for a few minutes, I realized that the letter was in the washing machine. There's what's left of the letter on the window sill." I pointed as I collapsed on the bed.

"Damn, you did have a rough morning," Trudy said, as she walked over to the letter. I then went into my backpack and took out the drawing that Levi had drawn and showed it to Trudy. "That looks just like you Kandee, this Levi dude is very talented," she said, as I put the picture on my desk and sat my thick dictionary on top of it. I wasn't trying to hide it; I was trying to get the creases out of the paper. I had already made my mind up about ironing the creases out, but the way my day was going, I couldn't risk it.

***

After breakfast, Trudy and I cleaned the kitchen since Aunt Joyce cooked. Her grits were a little thicker than the ones that I made, but everything else was good. The bacon was crispy, biscuits were buttery, and the eggs were fluffy. I took an Advil, with the remainder of my apple juice before I wiped down the counters and swept the floor. With Trudy and I cleaning the kitchen, it reminded me of Thanksgiving Day. As I started to think about mom, my eyes got watery. I remembered her in the kitchen cutting up the Turkey and bragging about how good I could cook.

As I tried not to let Trudy see me cry, I wiped my eyes with the drying towel. Just when I thought that Trudy couldn't see me, she asked, "Are you okay?" I took a deep breath and replied with a lie. "Sure, something got in my eye." "Oh. Didn't you say that this Levi guy rides your bus?" "Yeah, he does, he lives two stops away from here," I said, as I smiled at Trudy because I knew exactly what she was thinking.

After we had finished all of our chores, we asked Aunt Joyce if we could go for a walk and she said yes. We were going to ask dad, but he had left in the Suburban and hadn't come back yet. As we walked, we talked about why I was crying in the kitchen. Trudy put her arm around my shoulder, as I told her how much I missed my mom. Trudy suggested that I start writing in a journal. I liked the idea a lot and planned on doing that as soon as I got back home today.

When we turned the corner, I saw Levis house. His dad was outside washing his work truck. Along with the work truck, there was a gold Honda parked in the yard. "This is his house," I said, to Trudy as my heart began to beat faster. "Damn, is that his daddy? He is super fine; I know that Levi has to look good if he looks anything like his daddy" Trudy said, in a whisper. I elbowed her as we got closer to Levi's dad.

"Excuse me, is Levi here?" I asked before I gave my mouth permission to talk. As Levi's handsome father sprayed his work truck off, he replied, "You just missed him, he walked down to the corner store. If you walk fast, you may be able to catch up with him." "Okay, but if I don't catch up with him, can you please tell him that Kandee came by?" "Sure thing, baby girl," Levi's dad responded with a smile.

6

Sister Cousins

Trudy and I never caught up with Levi that day. We walked to the store, to the park, and then back home. As we turned the corner, we noticed that a lot of people were out and about in the neighborhood. For it to be December, the weather was perfect. Folks were in their rocking chairs or simply sitting on the steps enjoying the last few days of the mild weather. It felt great, it wasn't too hot or too cold.

When we walked up to the house, I saw that dad had returned. His Suburban was backed up in front of the house with the back doors wide open. My stomach begins to hurt after I looked inside and saw some of my mother's belongings that were stored in the attic for years. From where I was standing I only saw a few pieces of bulky furniture and a crate full of dusty porcelain dolls. I wasn't upset at all about them hauling off the scary looking dolls and not so much about the other items either. As long as no one was tossing out mom's clothes, I felt like I would be okay.

As we walked into the house, dad and one of his buddies from work made their way down the stairs with a long chalkboard. It was just as long as the one that was in Mrs. Warren's class at school. I wondered where that thing came from, as Trudy and I went to make some lunch. Thirty minutes later, lunch was served. Grilled cheese made with sourdough bread and tomato soup.

After the boys had eaten, they ran back down to the basement. I couldn't believe that they hadn't even been outside today. They loved being down there, and that was fine with me because they were out of my way. As Trudy and I went back for seconds, Aunt Joyce joined us in the kitchen. "What have you two been? You girls have been gone for over two hours" Aunt Joyce said. As I cleared my throat to tell her where we went, Trudy answered with a lie, "We only walked around the neighborhood a few times, that's it." "Okay, since both of you have your cycles now, you need to be careful about where you're going." "Yes ma'am," we said, in unison.

When we were done eating, Aunt Joyce called the boys from the basement to clean the kitchen. As the boys cleaned, Trudy and I watched *Family Matters*. I just love that Steve Urkel. I laughed and laughed until I overheard Dad and Aunt Joyce talking in the kitchen. I don't know exactly what was said, but I heard something about a check coming in the mail. I wondered what kind of check was coming, as Laura Winslow continued to insult Steve Urkel.

When *Family Matters* went off, Trudy and I went outside and sat on the porch. Trudy looked through a pile of magazines that dad was about to put in the Suburban and blurted, "I can do your hair like this." "Like what?" I inquired, as I looked over at the picture she held up. It was a lady that resembled Vivica Fox with synthetic braids that went down to her bra-strap. The moment I saw the braids, I wanted them instantly. After I snatched the magazine out of Trudy's hands, I ran up to dad and showed him the picture.

He had his hands full carrying an old mattress, but I didn't care. "Daddy, can I get my hair like this?" I begged as I shoved the magazine in his face. "Sure, as long as it doesn't cost me an arm and a leg," he said, as he slid the mattress into the back of his friends truck. "Thanks, Dad" I yelled, as I ran back on the porch. "Trudy, who can do my hair like this?" I asked as I looked at my boring reflection in the window. "I can do it; I did my friends hair like that before. I think that I may have some of the hair left too" said Trudy, as she ran in the house.

When she came back out, she had several packs of brownish colored synthetic braiding hair, a couch cushion, a hair tie, a lighter, and a comb. "Are you ready?" Trudy asked, as she smiled and walked towards me. "Yeah" I answered excitedly. After Trudy positioned the cushion in front of the chair that she was sitting in, I flopped down on it. She then tore open a pack of the synthetic hair and began to part my hair. "Eww, you need to wash your hair because you have a lot of dandruff." When I scratched my scalp and saw the flakes fall onto my black shirt and I agreed with Trudy.

"You're going to have to sneak and wash your hair because mom isn't going to let you." "How come?" I asked as I scratched my scalp some more. "Grandma say that when you have your period, you're not supposed to get your hair wet, they say it will make your cramps worse" explained Trudy, as I looked at the lady in the magazine. "I don't believe that crap," I said, as I got up off of the cushion. "Give me thirty minutes and I will be back with a dandruff free scalp."

After leaving Trudy on the porch, I quickly went into the hallway bathroom and locked the door. I searched under the sink for the dandruff shampoo. Mom made me wash my hair with this stuff before. It smelled bad, but it worked. I looked some more, and I found a bottle of Suave conditioner that smelled like coconuts.

I then turned the water on in the tub and dunked my head under the faucet. After making sure that my entire scalp was wet, I poured the sticky brown shampoo onto the top of my head and made enough lather to get rid of all of the dandruff flakes. When I dunked my head back under the faucet, my scalp started to tingle. That meant the dandruff shampoo was working. I was so excited to get those braids I almost forgot to condition my hair before I blow dried it.

Thirty minutes later, I grabbed a stack of magazines from the pile that was still sitting on the porch and sat down on the cushion between Trudy's legs. "Now this is an improvement," she said, as she parted my hair and began to braid. After the first two hours passed, I looked at all of the magazines that I grabbed off of the stack. Another hour passed and

I saw my dad and his friend make at least six trips to load stuff onto the truck and into the Suburban. Trudy and I talked about the things that we hadn't seen in years that were up in the attic.

By the time the fourth hour came around the sun was about to set and it was starting to get chilly. As I put my arms in my shirt to keep warm, I noticed that my butt was beyond numb and that I had to pee. Trudy told me that she only had one more row of braids to do, I decided that I could hold it. I squirmed as I smelled dinner cooking. Not just Aunt Joyce's dinner, but the neighbors too. Someone was frying some chicken, and I smelled jiffy cornbread baking. I wasn't sure who was cooking what, but I knew I was ready to eat.

"All Done" Trudy said, as she burned the last braid. I jumped up and ran to the bathroom and relieved myself. After I flushed the toilet, I turned the knobs on to wash my hands, and I finally looked in the mirror. Who was this beautiful girl staring back at me? It couldn't be me. As I stared and stared at myself, I admired my brown skin, high cheek bones, and long lashes. To me, I looked better than the lady in the magazine. As I looked at myself through a new set of eyes, I heard someone call me for dinner.

After I yelled, "I'm coming," I looked at myself for a few more seconds and brushed the hair off of my shirt. On the way to the kitchen, I heard the boys being loud and obnoxious. I rolled my eyes as I heard Aunt Joyce fussing at them and then I turned the corner. No one said anything; even the boys were speechless. "Pumpkin, your hair is beautiful," said Dad. "Kandee, you look like a doll, Trudy did an excellent job," Aunt Joyce added. "Thank you guys," I said, as I sat down at the table by Samuel.

"Is that really you Kandee? You looked like that picture of mommy when she was a teenager" said Rickey, as he bolted from the kitchen table. "Rickey, come back" Dad ordered. "I'm coming right back Daddy; he yelled from the den. When Rickey came back he was carrying a photo album; he pointed to the picture of mom when she was thirteen or so. Rickey was right; I looked just like my mother. After everyone had looked at the picture of mom, I felt proud. I couldn't believe that I had been this beautiful the whole time and didn't even know it.

When Trudy joined us at the table; we all said the grace and dug in, the fried chicken I smelled earlier was from our house, and so was the Jiffy cornbread. There wasn't any food left after we got up from the table. It didn't take long to clean up the kitchen; everyone helped. With the music pumping, I announced that I would make breakfast in the morning and the boys rejoiced as the asked for things like blueberry muffins, banana pancakes, and cinnamon buns. As I checked the pantry, I saw that we were in need of a few items and told dad that he needed to go to the grocery store.

After I wrote the grocery list, I handed it to dad, and turned the lights off in the kitchen. "That's a long list, I think I may need help at the store. Who wants to come with me?" Dad yelled as he leaned his head into the doorway of the basement. "Not me, that's boring," yelled one of the boys. After that, a chorus full of "No's" came from the basement and dad laughed. Aunt Joyce then said "I'll go with you if you don't mind. I have some things that I need to pick up myself." "Sure Joyce. I don't mind at all" he answered, before he cleared his throat and yelled down the basement stairs. "I want all of you knuckleheads washed and wearing clean underwear by the time I get back. Spray air freshener down there too, it stinks."

I added the air freshener to the end of the shopping list before Dad and Aunt Joyce left. They took his Suburban that was full of stick pins, magazines, and crates of old junk in the back. I didn't think that they were going to mess around while they were gone, but I wasn't 100% sure about that. As soon as I heard the Suburban leave, I tapped Trudy on the shoulder and told her to follow me. She followed me closely, as we went upstairs and stopped in front of dad's bedroom door.

"What are we about to do Kandee?" "We are about to be nosy," I said, as I turned the knob to dad's bedroom door. When I couldn't go in, I was surprised. The door was locked. After all of the years that I've been alive, I could never remember dad or mom locking their room door. He must have been hiding something. After we couldn't get into dad's room, we went to the next best place to get information from.

I held my breath, as I turned the doorknob to Aunt Joyce's room. I prayed that the door wasn't locked as it squeaked open. Aunt Joyce had only been in the room for a day and night, and she had transformed it already. The main thing I noticed was that the funky, stale odor that had always lingered in the room was no longer there. The smell of warm vanilla and honeysuckle made me feel relaxed. I adored Aunt Joyce's black four poster bed, as I counted all of the pillows that were lined up.

"Why does your mother have so many pillows on her bed Trudy?" I asked as I looked in her direction. "I don't know, she has always had a lot of pillows. She had more than that, but her boyfriend wouldn't let her take all of them when we left." As I counted seven, I wondered how in the world Aunt Joyce had any room to sleep on her full-size bed. While I continued to look around, I admired the picture on Aunt Joyce's nightstand. It was Mom and Aunt Joyce when they were little girls. Mom was holding Aunt Joyce in her lap while grandma smiled and leaned into the picture.

It seemed that Aunt Joyce loved my mom, but she had a crazy way of showing it. What woman in her right mind would knowingly sleep with a guy that her sister has been with? A no good, low down, snake in the grass like Aunt Joyce that's who. I wanted to take the picture and throw it up against the wall and let the glass shatter into a thousand pieces, but I didn't. I knew if I did that, Aunt Joyce would know that someone had been in her room.

"So what exactly are you looking for in here again?" Trudy asked as she opened one on her mom's dresser drawers. "Nothing, in particular, just being nosy I guess," I said with a giggle. "Eww, look at this." Said Trudy, as I turned in her direction. She held up a pink rectangle box that had naked men and women on the cover. "A nasty video! I shouted as I grabbed the box to get a closer look. My goodness, people actually do this?" I asked as I saw naked bodies covered in chocolate syrup and cool whip."

"I take it that you're still a virgin" Trudy said, as she put the VCR tape back in Aunt Joyce's drawer exactly how she found it. "Of course, I am.

Aren't you?" I asked, as Trudy pulled open another drawer and replied, "No." "What do you mean no?" I asked, as my heart skipped a beat. "I did it before. I had sex." "When? Where? And with who?" I asked. "It was last year, at a football game, and the guy was a senior" Trudy said, as she smiled. "You had sex at a football game?" I squealed with excitement. "Yeah and it felt good too."

With a puzzled look on my face, I asked, "So where did you guys do it? Under the bleachers?" "Child please, I have more class than that. We had sex in his mom's van" "In a van, that's classy alright. So how did the two of you pull this off?" I asked as I got comfortable on one of Aunt Joyce's pillows. "Well, the guy's mother was a teacher at the school we attended, she also worked at the concession stand on game nights" Trudy explained. "Wait a minute, did he get free drinks and candy? I know if my mom were alive and worked in a concession stand that she would give me free stuff" I commented, as I burst out laughing.

"Do you want to hear the story, or not?" Trudy asked, with a look of aggravation on her face. After had I stopped laughing, she continued. "Anyway, the guy's mother had an old van that reminded me of the one on the *Scooby-Doo* cartoons, minus the funky paint job. Her van was silver and red, and she adored it so much, that she parked it as far away from the event parking lot as possible. After someone accidentally backed into her van after a football game one night, she never parked in the event parking lot again." "So how did you guys get the keys?" I asked.

"She would give him the keys about thirty minutes before the game was over. I would walk with him to the van, and we would mess around. After we were done doing the nasty, he would park the van closer to the football stadium, and return the keys to his mom." "So, while his mom sold Air Heads and Ring Pops, you and her son were getting it on in her van?" I concluded. "Yep, I will never forget that night. The smell of his breath, the dampness of his skin, and the way he kissed me. Kandee, I swear I could melt right now. Just thinking about it still gives me the chills. "We did it a few more times after that, but I haven't heard anything from him since he left for college back in August" Trudy confessed, as she let out a deep breath. "Girl, we better get out of here, I'm sure Dad and Aunt Joyce will be back soon," I said, as I fixed the pillows on the bed. "You're right" Trudy agreed, as we high tailed it out of the room and back downstairs.

As soon as my foot crossed the threshold to the basement stairs, I yelled: "Time for you guys to start taking your showers." I heard three out of the four boys respond, by saying "Dang, I thought she forgot," "I'm not going first," and "Me either." As I shut the door to Funkville USA, I wondered why the boys didn't like taking showers or baths. I sure hoped that they would grow out of that nastiness soon, or they would never get a date.

While the boys took super quick showers, they left a trail of wet footprints through the house. Trudy and I tried to watch television, but nothing good was on. While we heard the boys fussing about who was wearing whose pajamas, Trudy and I laughed. "Kandee, I love your braids. I may braid my hair like that too. I think that there is enough hair left for me to do my hair tomorrow" she said, as she looked in the mirror on the doors of the coffee table. "You can braid your own hair?" "Yeah, but I may need you to help me with the braids in the back."

While Trudy and I carried on a conversation about the braids, we heard someone unlocking the front door. Rickey made his way through the living room and met dad at the door. He grabbed several bags of groceries out of his arms and walked towards the kitchen with them. I then heard dad's voice say, "Girls, we need your help. We ended up buying way more stuff than we intended." Trudy and I went outside in our bedroom shoes. As we approached the Suburban, we saw Aunt Joyce sitting in the front seat looking in the mirror on the visor. When she saw us coming, she closed it and got out of the truck. "We've got goodies for everyone, lots of *Little Debbie* snacks and even a giant bag of *Tootsie Rolls*," Aunt Joyce said, as she tugged at her skirt.

The wheels in my head were turning. I elbowed Trudy, and she gave me a look and shook her head. She knew exactly what I was thinking. As Aunt Joyce went into the house carrying three bags of groceries, Trudy opened the door behind the driver seat and looked around. "It smells like sex in here" she whispered. Just as Trudy began to say something else, dad startled her by yelling from the porch. "Trudy, all of the groceries are in the very back of the Suburban, not in the back seat." "Okay, Uncle Jack," she said, as she shut the door and walked to the back of the Suburban where I was.

***

After all the groceries were put away, I took a shower and went back downstairs with Trudy. We were the only ones in the den, Trudy popped an enormous bowl of popcorn on the stove. When the buttery aroma filled the house, the boys came out of the basement to grab a handful of popcorn. Before Samuel could even put his hand in the bowl, I said, "Go wash your hands and use soap." The look on my face must have frightened all of the boys because they all went to wash their hands.

I had to make another bowl of popcorn because the boys asked for more. While we all tried to agree on a movie to watch, Trudy went upstairs to see how many packs of synthetic hair she had left. After arguing for five minutes with the boys about them passing gas and not being able to decide on a movie to watch; I let them have the den and went upstairs to join Trudy. When I walked into her room, I saw four packs of braiding hair laying on top of the dresser. Trudy was digging through a box at the foot of her bed when I said, "Girl, those boys are disgusting. The whole den smells like popcorn and fart. Leave it to them to ruin a good time."

"I knew that you would be joining me up here soon after I heard all of that fussing" Trudy replied. "So do you have enough hair?" I asked as Trudy pulled three more packs of synthetic hair out of the box. "I do now." While Trudy took the hair out of the packs, I looked at myself in the mirror. I couldn't believe; this was me, and I looked as good as I did.

"Are you ready to learn how to do this?" "Yeah," I answered, as Trudy gave me a quick tutorial on hair braiding. When I finally understood how to add the synthetic hair with Trudy's hair, I was ready to rock and roll.

After Trudy got the radio from my room, she sat an old cracked mirror across from her and put her pillows on the floor in between my feet. An hour later and I had four rows finished. I couldn't believe that braiding was so easy. I started braiding the back of Trudy's hair while she started braiding from the front.

When my eyelids started getting heavy, I asked Trudy if we could finish her hair in the morning. "Girl, I was hoping that you would say that, because my hands are tired" Trudy replied, as she stood up and stretched. After we cleaned up the hair and packaging, I put on my night bonnet and went to bed. I quickly fell into a deep sleep until my bladder woke me up.

I crept out into the hallway to the bathroom to relieve myself. As soon as I sat on the toilet my bladder emptied and my stomach stopped hurting. After I flushed the toilet and washed my hands and went back to bed. After tossing and turning for almost an hour, my head began to hurt. The sad part is that I wasn't sure if it was hurting because I kept thinking about Levi or if it was from these damn braids. As much as I didn't want to leave my warm spot, I had to get a Tylenol out of the medicine cabinet.

I flung my blanket back and left the warmth of my bed and crept across the hallway to the bathroom once again. I didn't bother turning the bathroom light on because the *Ninja Turtles* night light did an excellent job of illuminating the medicine cabinet. While my eyes ran across all of the bottles in the cabinet, I heard a door creak open in the hallway. When I heard Aunt Joyce's voice, I closed the medicine cabinet quickly and stepped into the bathtub. Just as I quietly closed the floral shower curtain, the light came on in the bathroom.

"Are you trying to wake up the girls Joyce?" Dad said, in a whisper. "Of course I'm not, Jack. I think they should know. It's time, and I am tired of living like this" Aunt Joyce replied in a huff. "Well, can we at least wait until I sell this dump, and cash the checks before your family finds out about us and runs us out of town?" Dad asked, in a low, but stern voice. "Baby, people are already talking. Did you see the looks that we got in the grocery store this evening? Not to mention the looks the neighbors gave me when we were moving our stuff in the other day." Aunt

Joyce replied. "I don't want the kids to know that they are all siblings, not just yet. Let me figure this out, don't stress yourself about it Joyce" Dad advised.

After Dad and Aunt Joyce had gone into their separate sleeping quarters, I waited for what seemed like an hour before I pulled the shower curtain back and bypassed the medicine cabinet. Trudy was snoring something terrible when I entered her room. "Trudy, wake up," I said. After shaking for a moment, her eyes fluttered. "What's the matter Kandee?" She said as she yawned. "Did you know that we are sisters?" I asked as Trudy sat up in her bed. "What? What are you talking about? We're not sisters; we're cousins." "Well, according to the conversation that I just overheard between Aunt Joyce and Dad, all of us are brothers and sisters. You, Samuel, Rickey, Larry, Rich, and I." I said as I left Trudy's room in a huff. When I got back in the bed, I expected Trudy to enter my room at any moment, but she never did.

7

Change of Plans

The next morning Trudy woke me up by tapping me on my shoulder. My eyes fluttered and my mind immediately thought back to us being sister, cousins and my eyes popped open. "Wake up sleeping beauty. Did you forget about making breakfast this morning?" Trudy said as she flopped down on my bed. Breakfast was the last thing on my mind, as I looked at Trudy like she was crazy. Half of her hair was braided, and the other half wasn't. Before I could say anything, Trudy said, "Kandee, I had a crazy dream that you came into my room and told me that we are sisters. Anyway, what time are you going to help me finish braiding my hair?"

"Trudy, that wasn't a dream," "What? What do you mean it wasn't dream? Did that actually happen?" She shouted, as I got up and closed my bedroom door. "Shh, be quiet. You don't want them to hear you. Do you?" I said. "Of course, I don't want them to hear me. So what happened?" As I filled her in on the whole conversation I heard Aunt Joyce and Dad having last night, her eyes got bigger and bigger. As much as Trudy eavesdropped, she had no clue that all of us were brothers and sisters. I always wanted a sister, but I never imagined that I would get an older sister in the snap of a finger.

After Trudy had left my room, I wondered if mom had known about my cousins being my brothers and sisters. If she knew about dad and Aunt Joyce, I figured that she had to know about the additional children, but not necessarily. After about five minutes of some serious thinking, my brain felt fried. That's when I understood that there was no need for me to worry about mom. What she knew or didn't know, didn't mean anything now because she was gone and hopefully resting peacefully.

I felt a little emotional at the moment, but I kept my promise, and made breakfast. While the radio blasted Johnny Gill's *Rub You the Right Way*, my mood improved. As I measured the oil, flour, and sugar, Trudy mixed the ingredients together and poured them into baking pans. We were going to have apple muffins, banana pancakes, and cinnamon buns. I made sure that I left enough batter for tomorrow morning's breakfast because I wanted to take Levi a few muffins. The kitchen smelled like a bakery, and I was sure that the boys would appear out of the basement soon.

"It smells like heaven in here," Rickey said. "I can't wait to eat." Larry chimed in. "It won't be much longer," I said while I opened two packs of bacon. As the aroma of the pork filled the house, the rest of the family members joined us in the kitchen. When the timer went off, I took the muffins and cinnamon buns out of the oven and noticed that Aunt Joyce was sitting down in the chair that mom used to sit in. She usually said, "Good morning," but not today.

While I cracked the eggs into a huge skillet, I noticed the sour look on her face. Little did she know, I knew what the problem was, she was ready to bust a move and claim my daddy as her man. Too bad Dad said, "Not just yet." I laughed to myself, as I watched Trudy flip over the last four pancakes. After had I gotten the orange juice and milk out of the refrigerator, I saw my dad looking at Aunt Joyce. She was totally ignoring him and everyone else this morning, until she bit into one of my apple muffins.

"This is good Kandee; you did an excellent job. These muffins just seem to melt in my mouth." Said Aunt Joyce. "Thanks" I replied, as I grabbed a piece of bacon off of the plate in the center of the table. The more Aunt Joyce ate, the more she talked. When Rich and Samuel started talking with their mouths full of food Aunt Joyce blurted out, "Boys eat like your brothers are eating. Don't speak with your mouth full of food, that's not showing good manners." I kicked Trudy under the table, and she dropped her fork on the floor.

"Aunt Joyce, you said to eat like your brothers. You're so silly." Samuel said, as he laughed and continued to talk and chew with his mouth open. My heart dropped as my whole body got stiff. If it were possible, steam would have come out of dad's ears, the look on his face could have turned Aunt Joyce to stone if she had looked up at him. Instead, she excused herself from the table, as her face grew redder by the second. "What's wrong mom?" Larry yelled.

Aunt Joyce didn't answer Larry. I could tell that dad wanted to get up and run after her, but he fought the urge. Dad continued to eat in silence as Samuel said, "That would be so cool if you guys were my brothers, then you wouldn't have to move out, and we could stay in the basement forever." I could see dad losing interest in his meal as he pushed his plate away. "Boys I need you to show me how strong you are today. I need some help getting the rest of the stuff out of the attic." He said as he tossed the remainder of his food in the trash.

"Really Dad!" Rickey excitedly said. "Yes, now hurry up and eat so we can get the attic cleaned up by three. The pizza place downtown has a special that will end at five today, we may be able to go over and grab a few pies." "Pizza, I hope we can get one with lots of pepperoni." Said Samuel. As the boys ate the rest of their breakfast they talked about what kind of bugs and spiders that they might find up in the attic. They had totally forgotten about the brother conversation that they were having not even two minutes ago.

Since Aunt Joyce made such a dramatic exit out of the kitchen, Trudy and I were left to clean up the big mess. After the boys went back into the basement and dad went back upstairs, we whispered about what just happened. "I can't believe she said that," I said. "Now that was a close call. They are going to have to tell us soon." Trudy responded. "I wonder how the boys are going to react to this news. I know their little minds are going to be blown." I replied.

When the kitchen was spotless, Trudy and I headed upstairs to her room. After we shut the door, we talked about the whole sister- brother cousin thing. As Trudy got comfortable on her pillow, she asked, "What kind of check do you think Uncle Jack and mom are talking about?" "Maybe an insurance check from mom's death or maybe he's expecting his settlement check from when Samuel, slipped and fell inside of the grocery store last year." While we finished braiding her hair, we talked about where we might move and the possibility of us being rich.

As we daydreamed about having a bigger house, I realized that moving away meant that I wouldn't be able to sit with Levi on the bus anymore. "Trudy, I don't want to move. I don't want to leave Levi. I really like him, and I think that he likes me too." "Aww, maybe we won't move right away. Maybe the check will get held up in the mail or something." Replied Trudy. "I hope so, I don't want to leave this house. I can't believe that dad and Aunt Joyce are going to do this to us. Our family is never going to be the same again."

With all the chatter that Trudy and I were doing, we didn't realize that we finished her hair and that the both of us were sitting down for no reason. When Trudy got up, she stretched and looked into the big mirror attached to the dresser. While she pranced around in front of the mirror and swung her braids from side to side, I said, "You're going to break your neck if you keep on jerking it around like that." She paid me no attention as I gathered strings of synthetic hair off of the bed and floor to toss in the trash. "Oh my goodness, Kandee come here." Trudy gasped. After I tossed the stuff in the garbage, I went to see what Trudy wanted. With both of our eyes focused on the mirror we saw it, the resemblance was crazy. I don't know why we never noticed that we looked alike before.

It must have been the braids. Trudy and I looked so much alike that it was scary. "Holy Shit!" I said, as we both smiled at the same time. We looked like the sisters that we just found out we were. I was a few shades darker than Trudy. She was the color of a walnut shell, just like Aunt Joyce. Both of us had daddy's brown eyes, button nose, and long lashes.

The only difference was that I had my mother's high cheekbones and thin lips, and Trudy had dad's pointy chin and full lips.

After Trudy and I compared ourselves in the mirror, I asked her about her makeup. "I can show you how to put some on." Trudy happily suggested as she dug in her caboodle. I better ask dad first, I thought before I yelled, "Dad can I play in some of Trudy's makeup?" When I heard dad's muffled voice reply, "Yes, but not too much." I was the happiest girl in the world. In one weekend I got the sister that I always wanted and got permission to put on some makeup.

While Trudy showed me all of her makeup and explained what the purpose of everything was, I took notes. I watched her put a full face of makeup on and decided that this wasn't something that I wanted to do every day. "Can you put some of the stuff on my eyes, I don't want to put the powder on my cheeks and face," I said. "Sure, I'm going to show you what colors match best with your complexion," Trudy replied, as she pulled out a pencil case full of lipstick and lip gloss.

After an hour-long makeup tutorial, I felt like I knew everything there was to know about makeup. I knew how to take it off, re-apply it, and touch it up. Trudy even showed me how to make my thin lips look fuller, with a lip liner pencil. Now I was ready to go to the drug store and pick out my makeup. I hoped that daddy didn't think it was too much, I knew that mom would never let me wear all of this much eyeshadow.

As soon as we walked into the hallway, the boys were coming down from the attic. Larry yelled, "Y'all look like twins." "No, they don't." Said Samuel. "They do look alike," added Rickey as Aunt Joyce opened the door to her bedroom and peeked out. When she saw us standing in the hall, she closed her bedroom door, and we didn't see her anymore for the rest of the day. I figured she was sick to her stomach; she should have been for being so trifling. When dad came down from out of the attic, he said, "You two look lovely." That was all I needed to hear from him, from now on I was going to wear makeup.

Like dad promised, he took the boys to get pizza. When he asked if Trudy and I wanted to ride, we jumped at the opportunity to get out of the house. We loaded up the Suburban; I let Samuel sit in the front. The rest of us sat in the back seat and looked out of the window. When we passed by Levi's house, I saw him sitting on the steps. I thought that I would die, just from getting a glimpse of him made my palms sweat.

Before we went to the pizza place, we stopped at someone's house. After daddy blew the horn, a man came out and helped unload some things out of the back of the Suburban. The man then gave dad a fist full of cash and shook his hand before we left. When dad was hauling stuff off yesterday, I thought he was just taking it to the dump. I had no idea that he was selling it. I wondered how much money he had made off of the stuff in the attic and if he was saving money for us to hurry up and move? I made a mental note to tell Trudy about this and tried to think of a way I could get into dad's room with the lock on the door.

When we pulled up to the pizza place, there were hardly any parks. This place had the best pizza in town, and I couldn't wait to eat, but there was something I had to check on. As dad and the boys unloaded the Suburban, I messed around with my shoelaces until the coast was clear. When they were inside of the building, I jumped over the seat and looked inside the glove compartment and the arm rest for any important papers. All I found was a receipt from the tire place and a few old packs of ketchup from some fast food restaurant.

Just as I was about to get out of the car, I remembered to check the back of the Suburban for the stick pins. They were still there; I thought that they may have been displaced because of all of the stuff that had been in and out of the hatch. At the end of my investigation, Trudy asked, "What are you doing?" "I'm checking on my booby trap," I replied, with a giggle. "I don't even want to know," replied Trudy, as I shut the doors to the back of the hatch and walked towards the restaurant.

Trudy claimed that she didn't want to know about the booby trap, but she listened inquisitively as I told her about the stick pins. In the middle of one of her many questions, I blurted out, "Did you see Levi, when we passed by his house? He was sitting on his porch." "No, is that why you elbowed me in my ribs?" Trudy asked. "Yes," I replied, as I put my hand over my heart. "You got it bad for that dude; I can't wait to meet him." When we walked into the restaurant, we ended the conversation about Levi and sat down just in time to put in our drink order.

***

That night, I lay in bed and thought of ways to stop us from moving. Lord knows that I didn't want to leave Levi with his handsome self. As I drifted off, the thought of intercepting the mail came to my mind. If Trudy or I checked the mail every day and saw any important looking envelopes, we could open them to see what it was and toss it in the garbage if it was anything involving selling the house or a check. That was my only plan at the moment, but the wheels inside my head continued to turn as I went to sleep.

I was startled when the alarm sounded. I stretched and yawned before I turned the alarm off. When I walked into the hallway, I heard Trudy snoring from one direction and dad snoring from the other direction. Those two sounded like a bunch of Lumberjacks sawing down trees; I thought as I entered the hall bathroom and closed the door. When I sat down on the toilet, I saw that I wasn't bleeding anymore. I guess my period was gone. I was so happy that I decided to wear my white pants today.

After I washed my face and brushed my teeth, I went downstairs and started making breakfast. I retrieved the leftover apple muffin batter from out of the refrigerator and poured it into the muffin pans. All I could do was think about the look on Levi's face when he tasted one of my homemade muffins. I couldn't wait to get on the bus this morning. I almost jumped out of my skin as I thought of Levi seeing me with my new braids and makeup. I knew that he was going to ask me to be his girl. Today was definitely the day.

The moment after I put the muffin pan into the oven, I opened the door to the basement and yelled, "Get up." As soon as I heard movement and saw the glow of a light from down in the dungeon, I closed the door. The funk was unbearable; I don't know what those boys did down there

Kandee's Crush

all night. I took several deep breaths, as I went back upstairs to get ready. When I walked past the bathroom, I heard the shower running. That meant Trudy was up.

After I got dressed I went into Trudy's room. She was dressed in a long sleeve yellow shirt and a pair of super tight blue jeans. She looked great. I knew that a lot of guys were going to try to get her phone number today. As she complemented me on my white jeans and black shirt that read "NOT" across the front, I sat down on the side of her bed. "So are you nervous about going to a new school?" I asked. "Nope, not at all."

After Trudy fixed my makeup a little, I hustled back downstairs to check on the muffins. They were almost ready, so I boiled a box of sausage links and poured seven cups of juice. When the boys came into the kitchen, I looked each one of them over carefully. After asking them all if they washed their face, brushed their teeth, and if they have their deodorant on, I let them sit down at the table. I only had to send Rich back to the basement to put on his deodorant.

"Alright guys, you have twelve minutes to eat before the bus comes," I said, as Aunt Joyce walked into the kitchen fully dressed. "They aren't riding the bus this morning," said Aunt Joyce, as she poured a cup of coffee. "Why not?" I asked as dad came around the corner. "I have to register the boys at school; I figured that they would feel better if Rickey and Samuel could be with them." "Oh, I forgot about that," I said as I wrapped two muffins up in aluminum foil for Levi.

"You're not riding the bus either," said Dad. I thought that I would have a heart attack just like Fred Sanford; right there beside the pan of muffins. I felt like throwing a tantrum. Honestly, I didn't think that I could wait another minute. I wanted to see Levi right now. As I gathered my thoughts of throwing a tantrum, I sat down at the table and looked at Aunt Joyce. I wanted to slap the cup of coffee and the muffin out of her hand. I had lost my appetite and wanted nothing more than to run to the bus stop and get on bus 73.

By the time Trudy came downstairs, I was heading out the front door. "What are you still doing here?" She asked as I grabbed my backpack from off of the floor. "Aunt Joyce insists that I be there when she signs you up for school this morning." "That's crazy; I'm not nervous. You could have ridden the bus," Trudy replied. "Well, it's too late now," I said, as we both walked out onto the porch just in time to see bus 73 roll by.

As we all loaded into the Suburban, I wondered if Levi saw me when the bus passed by my house. I knew that all of those girls on the bus were happy that I didn't get on the bus this morning. I couldn't wait to bust their bubbles this afternoon with my new hair and makeup. I was going to sit with Levi, and I was going to sit by the aisle.

While Aunt Joyce and Dad registered Larry and Rich for school, Trudy and I waited in the Suburban. I warned Trudy about the people she shouldn't hang around at school and she took notes. I made sure I told her about this guy named Edwin. He was a senior, and he was the ultimate womanizer. Don't get me wrong, he was one of the flyest guys at our school. Most of the girls wanted him because he was popular, played football, tall, and handsome. There was a rumor going around that he had a baby already, but I didn't know how true that was.

When we saw Dad and Aunt Joyce walking back towards the Suburban, Trudy said, "I wonder what the two of them are going to do today with the house all to themselves?" "Gross. I don't even want to think about that" I hissed, as dad opened the door to the truck and got in. After we left the elementary school, we went to the high school. While Aunt Joyce filled out paperwork, I watched the clock like a hawk, it was almost 8:30. After the lady in the office gave Trudy her schedule and made a student identification card, she handed me a note to get to class.

While I showed Trudy around, some girl in the hallway said, "Hey Kandee, is that your sister?" I didn't know what to say. So I pretended that I didn't hear her and continued walking down the hall. As we approached the staircase, I saw Edwin coming down the stairs. I'm not sure if he paid me any attention, but he stared at Trudy so hard that he stopped walking and turned to watch her.

"Don't even look his way Trudy. He's trouble." I warned her. "Your first class is right here," I said, as I looked around for Trudy. She was nowhere in sight. I thought she was behind me. As I backtracked, I saw Trudy on the staircase talking to Edwin. When I called her name she jumped. "Trudy, your class is this way," I said as I pointed in the direction I had just come from. After Edwin wrote something down on a piece of paper, Trudy took it and stuffed the paper into the back pocket of her skin tight jeans.

I could have choked her, but instead of doing that, I showed her to class and walked as fast as I could to my homeroom. Before I opened the door, I took a deep breath and entered the class. Most people didn't even look up from what they were doing until Mrs. Warren said, "Good morning Kandee, do you have a pass to give me or are you tardy?" "I have a pass," I replied as I handed her the piece of paper.

When I sat down, I noticed that Levi wasn't even in his seat. While I wondered where he could be, I looked at the chalkboard. After I wrote down today's assignment, I got my notebook out of my backpack. As I started doing my work, Levi entered the classroom. I looked him dead in his face as he handed Mrs. Warren a pass and then sat down behind me. I wondered what he thought of my hair and if his dad told him that I came by the other day. I also wondered where he was coming from.

I felt someone tap me on the shoulder, and I hesitated before I turned around because I knew it was Levi. "Here's your book back," he whispered. I took the book without saying a word. After I finished most of my classwork, I cracked the book open to see a note on the inside. As much as I wanted to read the note, I couldn't risk it. I sat in the first row, and I couldn't get caught with a note. Mrs. Warren didn't play any games, and I sure didn't want her calling my daddy.

When there were only five minutes of class left, I finished up my classwork and turned it into Mrs. Warren. As other students started whispering, I cracked the book open and read the note:

Dear Kandee,

Why didn't you call me this weekend? After I drew that picture of you and poured all of my feelings into the letter on Friday, I thought you would have at least called me. I felt a connection between you and me, but I guess I was wrong. No girl has ever dissed me like you did. What's up with that? Write me back, please.

Sincerely Levi,

After I read the letter again, I quickly scribbled a note to Levi before the bell rang and I passed him back the book.

Dear Levi,

I'm so sorry. I do like you. I mean, I really really like you. I came to your house on Saturday, but your dad said that you went to the store. You wouldn't believe the weekend that I had. I'm going to have to tell you about it on the bus. Please don't be mad at me.

Sincerely Kandee,

While I waited for him to pass the book back to me, the bell rang. As I gathered my things off of my desk and reached for my backpack, I stood up. Levi then grabbed my hand and said, "Where's your next class? I want to walk you there if you don't mind." With a smile as big as the Joker's, I replied, "Oh, I don't mind at all. It's downstairs."

8

Puppy Love

I watched the clock on the wall like a hawk as the second hand got closer and closer to the twelve. When the bell rang, I got out of my seat so fast that you would have thought that the fire alarm sounded instead of the bell. I made my way through the hall and I saw Levi standing by the water fountain. That's exactly where he said he would be when the school day was over. When I finally reached him, he took my purple backpack and the book I had in my arms.

"Thanks, Levi." "No problem," he replied with a smile. As we walked towards bus 73, I saw Trudy talking to Edwin. As much as I didn't want to leave Levi's side, I had to get her away from him. "Levi, can you wait right here for a second? I've got to make sure my cousin knows which bus to get on." Before Levi could say anything. I walked over to Trudy and said, "Excuse me, Edwin. Trudy, you need to come on. The bus will be leaving in a minute." "Watch out little sis, I can give your big sister a ride home. My car is right around the corner."

I was going to ignore his arrogant ass, but I didn't. I couldn't let him just try to push me to the side and get into Trudy's pants. With all the attitude I could gather, I said: "Trudy doesn't want to ride in your hoopty, she's getting onto bus 73 with me, and I'm not her sister, I'm her cousin." "Why so much attitude Lil' sis? You can't fool me; even a blind man could see that you two are sisters. Now go away, I'll send Trudy to bus 73 in a minute." Said Edwin, as he shut me down.

On my way back to bus 73, I wondered why I didn't cuss Mr. Rico Suave out. I thought about turning around to complete the task at hand, but I decided not to because I didn't want to leave Levi waiting any longer. When I got back in line for the bus, Levi asked, "Is she coming?" "Yes, as soon as she's done talking to that jackass." Levi burst out laughing. "I never heard you cuss before; you must be really upset." "Something like that" I replied, as I stepped onto the bus.

When we got to our seat, I sat by the window. Levi handed me my backpack as he got comfortable. "Did I tell you that I like your braids?" He asked as I looked out of the window to see what Trudy was doing. "No, you didn't. Thank you." I said as I blushed. As more people got onto the bus, I wondered if Trudy did want to ride home in Edwin's hoopty. I decided that I wouldn't worry with Trudy and Edwin, and focused my attention on Levi.

"Tell me about your weekend" Levi said, as he took his hand and tucked one of my braids behind my ear. After my brain had registered the connection of Levi's hand and my earlobe, I felt like I could have melted. It was December, and I wanted to put the window down on the bus because his one touch made me hot. After that, I forgot about Trudy and gave Levi 100% of my attention. As the bus started to roll, I told him how much I loved his drawing. And by the time the bus was off of the campus, I told him about my aunt and cousins moving in with us.

At the stop sign down the street, I told Levi about accidentally washing the letter. Then I told him how I tried to let it dry on my window sill. He laughed and said, "Dang, that's a lot. So were you able to read any of the letter?" "No, I didn't. Can you tell me what you wrote in the letter?" I asked. "Umm, let me see if I can remember, I had a long weekend too you know."

I playfully slapped Levi on the thigh as he continued to talk. "I remember that my phone number was in the letter, and I asked you if you would go out with me. That was after I told you how pretty you were." "Are you serious Levi? You want me to be your girlfriend?" I asked, as I

Kandee's Crush

nearly swallowed my gum. I had to be dreaming. I absolutely could not believe this. I guess I was kind of loud because the girl that sat two seats in front of us turned around and rolled her eyes at me.

"Yes, I'm serious. Kandee, you are the only girl at this school that hasn't thrown yourself at me. I don't want to be with any of those girls and I've honestly been checking you out since the morning you thought that I was in the wrong seat." He confessed as I stared at him. I thought I'd said, "I can't believe this shit" inside of my head, but I actually said it out loud. "Why can't you believe this? You're beautiful and seem to be a nice person; I would love to get to know you better. You know, outside of the bus and this seat," he said with a chuckle.

"Oh my goodness! Did Levi just call me beautiful?" I said, to myself as I took a deep breath. "Okay, I'll be your girlfriend, but only if you promise not to take notes from any more girls." "It's a deal." Levi agreed, as he dug in his backpack and handed me three notes. "You wrote these for me?" "Nah, some girls gave me those in the bus parking lot, whenever you went to get your cousin."

I frowned up my face as I balled the letters up. Levi laughed, then got a pen out of my trapper keeper and reached for my hand. As he moved the pen back and forth, I saw that he was writing his phone number on my palm. "Call me today, anytime," He said, as he gathered his things and walked towards the front of the bus. I was in such of a daze that I wondered where Levi was going. I didn't even realize that the bus had stopped in front of his house.

I'll tell you what I did realize, though. Trudy, my sister-cousin wasn't on the bus. After stretching my neck like an ostrich, I didn't see a head on the bus that looked like mine. I saw a ponytail, finger waves, bushy Afro, curly Afro, and one French braid. There were no other box braids in sight, other than mine. I was supposed to be on cloud nine, now that I was officially Levi's girlfriend. But I couldn't even enjoy that because of Trudy and that slime ball Edwin.

The bus came to a stop in front of the curve near my house, and three girls got off of the bus before I did. I looked at Levi's number in my hand and got butterflies in the pit my stomach. I couldn't wait to call him and see how his voice sounded on the phone. While I daydreamed about Levi, I heard a voice from behind the bushes ask "How was your bus ride?" To tell you the truth, I was startled, but when I realized that it was Trudy, I got an attitude.

As she walked out from behind an overgrown bush in one of our neighbor's yards, I stopped dead in my tracks and said, "Why didn't you ride the bus? I was really worried about you." "Don't get your panties in a bunch, Edwin gave me a ride home," She answered as we got closer to our house. "I hope you don't ride with him again, I heard that he can get real frisky and that he doesn't understand the word No."

When I saw one of the neighbors checking their mail, I remembered that I was supposed to be intercepting the mail so we wouldn't have to move right away. After I looked in the driveway and saw that Dad and Aunt Joyce's car was gone, I ran to the mailbox. "Is anything in there?" Trudy asked as she waited for me on the porch. "No, just junk mail." When the thought of Edwin crossed my mind again, I asked, "Did you tell him that we were sisters Trudy?" After she didn't reply, I knew that she had told him. "Trudy. Did you tell him?" I yelled as I yanked her by the arm. "Yeah, I told him, but he said that he wouldn't tell anyone," she replied, as she looked down at her notebook.

After I took a deep breath, I said, "You can't go around telling people that I'm your sister. The last thing we need is for this to get out. I don't want to be the laughingstock of the entire high school." "I'm sorry; I swear that he already knew. He said that we had to be more than cousins because we looked too much alike and…" "You know what Trudy, I don't want you to ruin the rest of my day by telling me anything else that Edwin said." "Can I bask in the ambiance of getting Levi's phone number and becoming his girlfriend?"

"Girlfriend!" Trudy said, as she grabbed me by my shoulders and shook me. "You're his girlfriend? Damn, I should have been on the bus." She continued to talk loud until she opened the entry door to the house. To our surprise, the boys were in the den watching television. I smelled something cooking, but I remember I didn't see Aunt Joyce's car outside.

Kandee's Crush

"Who's cooking?" I asked as I hurried into the kitchen. "I think the crop pot is on," said Samuel.

"Samuel, it's called a crock pot, not a crop pot." Trudy said as she joined me in the kitchen. "Did you hear him Kandee? He called the crock pot, a crop pot." I laughed, as I looked to see that not one, but two crock pots were spitting steam. After reading the note on the counter that read: "Don't eat the chicken, eat the soup." I opened the lid on one pot. My mouth watered as I saw huge pieces of juicy chicken and chunks of stewed onions. In the other pot, I saw chunks of vegetables and ground beef. The aroma smelled so good that I wanted to take a spoon and eat right from the pot.

I hadn't eaten at lunch because I didn't want to eat in front of Levi. As my stomach growled, I almost washed my hands before I remembered that Levi's phone number was there. I opened the junk drawer by the sink and pulled out a dull pencil. Then I copied the number down on the back of an old envelope. After that, I slid the envelope in my back pocket and washed my hands. "Trudy, will you remind me that I put Levi's number in my pocket?" I asked as I washed my hands. "Yeah, only if you remind me; to remind you." She chuckled

I used an entire loaf of bread to make peanut butter sandwiches to go with the soup. When the sandwiches were piled up on a plate, I told the boys to go and wash their hands so they could eat. They must've been hungry too, because I only had to tell them once. After everyone had a seat, we ate without saying the grace. Before I remembered, I was on my second bowl of soup. Rickey realized that we didn't say the grace about the same time I did. "Kandee, we forgot to pray over our food," He said. "It's okay Rickey, when you say your prayers tonight, don't forget to thank God for the food," I replied as I winked my eye at him.

***

By the time 6:30 rolled around, Dad and Aunt Joyce still weren't home. Trudy and I made sure that the boys took a bath, did their homework, and brushed their teeth. After they were squeaky clean, they all went down in the basement, and we didn't hear another peep out of them. While Trudy talked on the phone with that good for nothing Edwin; I did my homework and took a shower. I also gathered my clothes to wear to school tomorrow. I wasn't sure if I was going to get to call Levi tonight or not. Trudy had been on the phone with Edwin for almost two hours, and it didn't look like he was going to get off anytime soon.

She was comfy cozy, laying on the couch with a pillow and everything. As soon as I got a piece of paper out my desk to write Levi a letter, I heard Trudy say, "Oh, okay. I'll see you in the morning. Sweet dreams." My heart skipped a beat when I heard her hang up the phone and go to the bathroom. After she had closed the door, I knocked and asked, "Are you done with the phone? I'm about to call Levi." "Yeah, I'm done. Edwin's mom had to use the phone."

"Yes." I thought to myself, as I went downstairs to the phone. I lay in the same spot where Trudy had just gotten up from. After I picked the phone up, I realized that the number was inside of my pants pocket. I thought that I remembered the number, but after dialing the wrong number twice, I got up and went upstairs to get the paper out of my jeans. When I passed by the bathroom again, I heard Trudy singing in the shower. Her voice was amazing and crystal clear. If I could sing like that, I would sing in the shower too.

When I went back downstairs, I got comfortable on the couch and dialed Levi's number as I looked at the piece of paper. After the phone rang twice, someone answered and said, "Hello." "Hi. May I please speak to Levi?" I asked. "Just a second" the voice responded, as I heard them yell for Levi to pick up the phone. "What took you so long to call me?" He asked. "I bet you don't even know who this is" I replied. "Yes, I do. This is the same person who washed my letter in the washing machine and put it on their window sill to dry."

"Ha ha, very funny," I said, as I got serious. "Hold up, before we get any deeper into this conversation, give me your number right now. I can't wait around for you to call me every day. I need to be able to get in touch with you when I want to." Levi urged. "Alright, I responded," as I called my number out to him. "So what have you been up to since we got off of the big yellow taxi?" He asked. As I told him everything I did, he listened. I had his full attention, and he had mine. We talked for hours and hours before I got sleepy. The last thing I remembered hearing Levi say was that he loved corn beef hash.

I don't know what time Dad and Aunt Joyce came in, but there was a blanket over me when I woke up a little after five in the morning. I didn't remember telling Levi good night or good-bye. As much as my body told me to go back to sleep, I didn't do it. With my mind on Levi, I quickly dialed his number and prayed to God that his dad didn't answer the phone. When Levi answered, he didn't sound like he was asleep at all.

"Hello," he answered. "Did I wake you?" I asked as I sat up on the couch. "Nope, my dad just left for work, his alarm woke me up, and I can't go back to sleep. I was about to iron my clothes for school and fix a bowl of cereal." "Oh, what time did we get off of the phone?" I asked as I covered my mouth to hide the yawn. "About eleven, I was talking and you never said anything. After calling your name a few dozen times, I realized that you were asleep. So I hung up." "I'm sorry." I apologized. "That's okay Kandee," He replied.

Levi and I talked until I heard dad's alarm clock go off. When I heard him start moving around upstairs, I washed my face and started breakfast. Grits, corn beef hash, and eggs were on the menu. I had the meal cooked in no time and was upstairs getting ready by the time Trudy even woke up. When I sat down at my homework desk to put a little makeup on and some of mom's favorite perfume, Trudy popped in my bedroom. "You got it, girl, you look like a superstar," She said, as she went into my closet and grabbed my sweater with a picture of Prince on the front. "You're only saying that because I let you borrow my favorite shirt."

"No seriously, you look great. Hey, how did you fall asleep on the phone last night? Girl, you were snoring and everything when I put the phone on the hook and threw a blanket on top of you." Trudy said. "You better be lying, I hope I didn't snore in Levi's ear," I replied, as I got up from the desk and grabbed my backpack. "Oh, what time did you come downstairs last night? I'm trying to figure out what time Dad and Aunt Joyce got back home." "Ummm, after I tucked you in on the couch, I called Edwin back and talked to him for another hour, so it had to be after twelve."

"What in the hell could they have been doing, hanging out in the streets that late? Do you think that they were at a motel?" I asked. "I don't know Kandee, don't worry about those old folks, what they're doing will catch up with them sooner or later," Trudy replied, as we both walked into the kitchen. Dad was already at the table drinking a cup of coffee, and the boys were sitting down eating. "Kandee, did you pack my lunch yet?" Dad asked. "No, I'm going to in a second," I replied. "I will fix it," said Aunt Joyce, as she came from around the corner. She was glowing and looked like she was on cloud nine. "Okay, Thanks, Aunt Joyce."

When everyone was finished eating, I grabbed a Styrofoam cup and layered the grits, eggs, and corn beef hash into it. "I knew that Levi was going to enjoy this." I thought to myself as I put some foil over the top of the cup. Since I was running out of time, I didn't have a chance to clean up the kitchen. Hopefully Aunt Joyce would clean it since she was in such a great mood.

After waiting with the boys at their bus stop, we walked to our bus stop and waited for bus 73. As we talked, puffs of white clouds came from our mouths. It was freezing, I should have worn a coat today. As I stood there with my backpack on my back, I used the cup of grits to keep my hands warm. "Trudy, are you riding the bus home today?" I asked. "I'm not sure yet, I will let you know before the bus leaves this afternoon." I started to ask her another question, but I changed my mind when I saw the bus approaching.

As soon as I stepped on the bus, I got the feeling back in my face. When I looked towards our seat, I saw Levi and butterflies were in the pit of my stomach. He slid over as I walked closer to our shared seat. "You sure do smell good." Thinking that he was referring to my perfume, I replied, "Thanks." "So, what did you cook this morning? You smell like food." "Here you go," I said, as I handed him the cup of grits, eggs, and corn beef hash. "What's this?" He asked, as I opened my pencil case and handed him a napkin and a plastic spoon. "That's your breakfast," I said, with a smile.

"Are you serious?" "Yes, I remembered you saying something about some corn beef hash last night," I replied, as Levi took the foil off of the cup. After he had peeked inside of the cup, he said, "Kandee, you are the best." Then he grabbed my face and kissed me on the cheek. Before he could start eating, I grabbed his face and turned it towards mine and kissed him back. I didn't know what had gotten into me.

After my first kiss ever, I watched him eat and I admired his dimples. As he ate spoonful after spoonful, he talked to me, but I didn't hear a thing he said. All I could do was think about the kiss that we just shared. His plump lips felt like the softest cotton that I ever felt. From this day forward I knew that I would always have the hots for him. It was going to take a lot for me to come down off this natural high.

When bus 73 pulled into the parking lot at the school, everyone stood up to get off of the bus. As Levi stood close behind me, I could feel his body heat. I loved the way he felt, and I wished that I could have stayed pressed up against him for the rest of the day. Too bad Levi left me when we got off of the bus. "I will catch up with you when we get to class," he said before he walked away and stood with some of his friends. If I didn't say that my feelings were hurt right now, I would be lying.

I watched Levi from afar until I heard Denise yell my name. She was standing all alone near a brick column. As I walked towards her, Trudy followed me. Before I could introduce Trudy to Denise, Denise said, "You guys look alike." "I know," I said. After I had introduced them to each other, Denise asked, "Is this the cousin that you needed help getting in touch with last month?" "Yeah, that's her" I answered, as I kept an eye on Levi.

Just as I started telling Denise about me and Levi being boyfriend and girlfriend, Trudy spotted Edwin and left. I continued to tell Denise about the drawing, letter, and the phone conversations. She was just as excited as I was and couldn't believe that I made a move on Levi on the bus this morning. After Denise and I shared a few more secrets, the bell rang.

By the time I got halfway to class, Levi had caught up to me and grabbed my hand. When he latched fingers with me, I wanted to melt down into a puddle of nothing. I couldn't believe that Levi and I were walking down the hallway holding hands. If looks could kill, I would be dead. So many girls shot imaginary arrows in my direction that it was ridiculous. I held my head high as we entered the classroom, with Levi by my side nothing could phase me.

Mrs. Warren didn't let us work with partners today. She had a real nasty attitude. She must've been on her period or something. While I tried to focus on the assignment that was written on the board, I felt my eyelids getting heavy. When the bell rang it was a bittersweet feeling because I was ready to leave, but I was going to miss Levi. Before he walked me to my next class, he gave me another note.

As I walked into my next class and saw a television on a rolling cart, I knew that we were watching something boring. I hated history. After the teacher took attendance and turned on the video about World War 2, I propped my head up on my arm and drifted off. I was startled when someone tapped me on my shoulder. It was the teacher, and he didn't look happy. After I sat up and stretched a bit, I started taking notes. When the bell rang, I gathered my things and headed towards the exit. I didn't make out of the room before the teacher called me back.

A few girls laughed at me as they rolled their eyes and left the class. I heard one say "Hey Levi." as I stood by the teacher's desk. "If you fall asleep in my class again young lady, you're going to get lunch detention. This is your first and last warning." The teacher warned. "Yes sir," I said, as I left the classroom. When I turned the corner I saw Levi; he was just standing by the water fountain. "What took you so long?" He asked as I handed him my books. "I fell asleep in class and got chewed out by the teacher." He then chuckled and asked, "Did you dream about me?"

9

Losing It

After one week of holding hands, everyone at school knew that Levi and I were a couple. It seemed as though I had become popular overnight. Everyone knew my name, and they knew that if they saw Levi, I wasn't too far behind. While our phone conversation grew longer and deeper, so did our kisses. I messed up big time when I started focusing more on Levi and less on my school work. After I had failed two tests back to back, I made up an excuse about not being focused because of mom's death. I knew I was wrong for that, but if dad found out I was making bad grades because of a boy, he would put me on punishment.

Being in love and battling my hormones was a job in itself. As the last days of school before Christmas break dwindled away, I wondered how I would deal without seeing Levi every day. Trudy and I already had a phone schedule worked out, so I knew I would get to talk to him. We each used the phone for two hours, and then we switched. So far it was working out good. While Trudy was on the phone, I usually did my chores and homework.

I knew that I had it bad for Levi, but Trudy was hooked on Edwin in another way. She only met him last week, and they were already having sex. I warned Trudy several times and insisted that she be careful. Usually, after Edwin rocked a girl's world a few times, he would leave them an emotional wreck. I saw a few of Edwin's ex-girls crying in the cafeteria and some even sadly watched Edwin from afar as their friends gathered around them and gave Edwin dirty looks. While Edwin paid no attention to his ex or their friends, he pursued his next victim.

Everyone at school knew that Edwin was a womanizer and that he used his good looks and hoopty to get what he wanted from girls. I don't know why girls were so easy to give it up to a guy like Edwin. I guess he was just smooth like that, whatever the case - I sure hoped that Levi wasn't like him.

I hoped Trudy knew what she was doing, moving fast with a guy never lead to a good outcome. At least that's how it always ended in the movies and with Edwin's previous relationships. Since Trudy enrolled at my school, she'd only ridden the bus home one time. I wondered where they went in the afternoons and how they did it so fast. I wanted to ask her, but I knew she would end up telling me in due time.

***

When the last day of school before winter break came, I was feeling a little emotional. I was glad I would get a break from school, but I was going to miss sitting with Levi on the bus. While Levi and I walked to class, I held his hand tightly. Other than on the bus this afternoon, I didn't know when the next time I was going to be able to hold his hand again. I knew that we were going to be out of school for a little over two weeks. I had to think of a way to see him over the winter break.

Other than being worried about missing Levi over winter break, school was actually fun that day. The teachers didn't assign any assignments. In Ms. Warren's class the only thing we did was see how many words we could make out of "Merry Christmas." We even got to work in groups and of course Levi and I worked together. In my next two classes we watched movies and in my last period class we had a party.

Before the bell rang, the principal made an announcement about making the right choices and drinking and driving. While he rambled on and on, the students continued to eat and drink. As the teacher walked around with a trash bag collecting our trash, a thought entered my mind. "What if Trudy and I went over to Levi's house one day during our winter break." If we went over to his house before, we could probably walk back over there again. When the bell finally rang, most of the students left their trash on their tables.

I couldn't leave the teacher to clean up this mess by herself; so I quickly helped her and sprinted to the bus parking lot. As soon as I walked out of the door, I saw Trudy walking with Edwin. When she saw me she yelled, "I'm not riding the bus today." "Okay." I said, as I talked to Denise. "I heard that Edwin had sex with the co-captain of the varsity cheerleading squad." She said. "I believe it, and I'm not surprised at all," I replied. "So what are you guys doing over winter break?" Asked Denise, as she waved at one of her other friends. "I don't know, probably a bunch of nothing. I'm kind of upset about not being able to see Levi. I'm really going to miss him." "Maybe my mom will let me stay the night with you one night, if she does we can think of a way to for you to sneak out and see Levi." Denise said, with a naughty grin. "I like the way you're thinking. I'm going to call you tomorrow." I said, as Levi walked up and took my hand.

Levi greeted Denise, and we walked hand in hand to the bus. After we got into our seat, I continued to hold his hand. This was the first time I ever held his hand while the bus was in motion. "What's up with you Kandee?" He asked as I put my head on his shoulder. "I'm a little sad because I'm going to miss you over the holiday." "Aww, for real. We'll get to talk on the phone every day; we aren't going anywhere because my dad has to work," Levi replied. "Do you think we might be able to see each other during the break?" I asked, as I lifted my head up and looked into his eyes. "I'm sure we could; my dad works from 8 am until 5 or 6 in the evening." "Well my dad works the same hours as your dad, but my Aunt Joyce is looking for a job. I hope she gets one soon, that way I will be able to come over." With a brighter outlook about winter break, I released his hand and reached in my backpack to get a letter I had written to him.

When I gave him the letter he smiled and opened it up. As he read, I blushed and put my head back down on his shoulder. We sat in silence from then until it was time for him to get off of the bus. Before he got up, he kissed me on my cheek and made his way to the exit. After I slid over to his spot, I let out a deep breath and looked out the window. I missed him already.

After I got off of the bus, I looked at the bush where Trudy usually stood and she wasn't there. I decided to wait for her for a few minutes, but she never came. "Come on Trudy. Where in the hell are you?" I said to myself, as I started walking towards the mailbox. I was happy to see that Aunt Joyce wasn't home, as I heard footsteps running up behind me. "Kandee, wait up." "What happened, why were you late?" I asked as I stood there with my arms crossed. "Girl, it's a long story. I will tell you later, I have to go take a shower." Trudy said as she passed by me with her skirt twisted.

***

Later that night, Aunt Joyce and Dad came home around the same time. The meatloaf with extra tomato paste was just coming out of the oven when dad walked through the door. I didn't care at all that dad's fly was unzipped or that Aunt Joyce had a hickey on her neck. I'd talked on the phone with Levi for almost three full hours, and I was beyond happy. As we all sat down at the dinner table, Aunt Joyce told everyone about her interview at the nursing home uptown. Deep down inside I hoped that she got the job. I wanted Aunt Joyce out of here in the daytime, so I could spend some time with Levi without her asking me where I was going.

I had to wake Trudy up from her nap and tell her that it was time to eat. After she had gotten out of the shower earlier, she went to her room to lay down. I hadn't seen her since; I didn't go looking for her either because I didn't want to get off of the phone with Levi. With sleep lines fresh on her face, she joined us at the dinner table. As she piled homemade mashed potatoes, meatloaf, and sweet peas onto her plate, I wondered what she and Edwin had done today after school.

When the boys went back down into the basement, I volunteered to clean the kitchen. While I ran the dish water in the sink and hummed along to the radio, I wasn't paying Aunt Joyce and Dad any attention. That was until I heard Aunt Joyce say, "I wonder if that check is going to come next week?" "They guy from the company said that the check should arrive by next Friday," Dad said as he stuck his fork into the last piece of meatloaf.

After Aunt Joyce and Dad left the kitchen, I made a mental note to check the mail, as I put all of the food away and washed the dishes. When I was done, I plopped down on the couch in the living room and picked up the phone. I heard a dial tone and happily dialed Levi's number. We talked for two more hours before I ended the call. Talking about absolutely nothing with Levi made me yearn to be closer to him. "I wish I would have known him a long time ago." I thought to myself, as I hung up the phone I went upstairs to talk to Trudy.

"You know that you aren't supposed to lay down on a full stomach Trudy." I fretted, as I entered her room without knocking. "I can't help it, all I want is do is lay down. Girl, Edwin wore me out today." Trudy replied, as she got up and closed her door. "How could he wear you out if you were only with him for thirty minutes?" "Edwin and I skipped school today." "How did you skip school? I saw the both of you guys walking together at the end of the day." I replied. "We came back to the campus to get his gym bag out of his locker, he didn't want to leave the stinky bag in there for the entire winter break."

"Are you serious Trudy?" "Of course, we went to Edwin's grandparent's house. They're both retired and are always gone. Anyway, Edwin has an extra key, he waters his grandmother's plants for her." Trudy added as she sat up on the bed. The wheels turned inside of my head. "Trudy, I want to spend some time with Levi. I want to go to his house one day next week when his dad is at work." "Say no more, I was thinking about sneaking out one night to be with Edwin. If you can help me out, I will make sure that I keep mom and the boys occupied. They won't even know that you're gone."

"That sounds great. I hope that Aunt Joyce gets that job, that way she and dad will be gone all day." "The way she talked about how good the interview went, it seems like she already has it. Let's sleep with our fingers crossed tonight." Trudy replied, as we both smiled. "Oh, did you check the mail today?" She asked as she rearranged her braids in the mirror. "No. I was about to check the mail after I got off the bus, but you sidetracked me when you ran up behind me. We need to stay on top of our game with that because I heard Dad and Aunt Joyce talking about a check tonight while I cleaned the kitchen." "You're right, Kandee." She agreed.

After I left Trudy's room, I went into my room and got my night clothes out. After I took my bath, I lay on my bed and hugged one of my pillows. I pretended that it was Levi. I couldn't wait to spend some time alone with him. As I wondered what we would do, thoughts of movies I could take over to his house crossed my mind.

***

The next morning when I woke up, the familiar scent of my mother filled my bedroom. After I stretched and yawned a bit, I opened my door to see a hallway filled with my mother's things. There were piles of clothes, boxes of shoes, garbage bags filled with her underclothes, and even mom's dresser. I felt as if I would transform into *The Incredible Hulk* as I saw Aunt Joyce and Dad dragging out the trunk that held my mother's fancy church hats.

"What in the hell do you two think you're doing? Why are you pilfering through mom's things? She hasn't even been dead three weeks, and you're getting rid of all her stuff. I can't believe you, daddy." I screamed. After the short moment of silence, I heard the bathroom door creak open, and Trudy peeked her head out. Dad dropped his end of the trunk before he said, "Now wait a damn minute missy. I know you're emotional about losing your mother, but you will not raise your voice and cuss at me in my house."

When the words "Go to hell flew out of my mouth." I knew that I had gone too far. As dad took three gigantic steps towards me, I knew I should have ran, but I froze up and couldn't move at all. When his hand came in contact with my cheek, I felt a horrible sting and stumbled back a few steps. "Jack, leave the poor girl alone. She's emotional; she misses Rita, don't punish her for speaking her mind." Aunt Joyce said as she whisked me away to the safety of my bedroom.

After falling onto my bed and bursting out into sobs, I yelled more obscenities to dad from the safety of the closed door. "Let it out honey, it's okay. I know you miss your mom. I miss her too." I did just what she said, only to hear heavy stomping on the stairs, a door slam, and the rumble of the muffler from the Suburban. After I calmed down, Aunt Joyce gave me a hug, and it felt pretty good. Almost like the hugs my mom used to give me.

"How about we go through the rest of your mom's things together?" Aunt Joyce suggested as she handed me another piece of tissue. "Alright," I said. When we went back into the hallway, Trudy was standing by my bedroom door. She probably was eavesdropping, but I didn't care because she already knew all of my secrets.

After we all had gone through most of my mother's things, we each had a few new pieces to add to our wardrobe. I got a few sweaters and all of her accessories and perfumes. Trudy picked out a few scarves and belts, and Aunt Joyce picked out three of her dresses. Almost two hours passed while we looked through mom's things, I was in a good mood, but my nerves got the best of me when I heard the Suburban pull up in the driveway. I don't know who got out of the hallway faster, Aunt Joyce or Trudy.

With me standing at one end of the hallway and dad standing at the top of the stairs, it looked like we were in one of those westerns that mom used to watch on Saturday afternoons. After both of us looked at each other long and hard, he broke the silence. "Pumpkin, I shouldn't have hit you, but I won't allow you to be disrespectful towards me or any other adult. That's not the way you were raised." "I know and Daddy, I'm sorry. I won't ever do that again." I responded, as I walked past mom's trunk full of hats and gave him a big hug.

After we made up, Trudy and Aunt Joyce joined us in the hallway, and we finished going through the rest all of mom's stuff. Then dad called the boys to help carry a few things out to the Suburban. When the hallway was clear and the boys were back down in the basement. Dad and Aunt Joyce stood on the porch and talked. It looked like they were deep in thought about something and I wondered what in the hell they were talking about.

When I pressed my ear against the entry door, I couldn't hear a thing, so I went out the back door and listened to them from the side of the house. "We should be able to get a few hundred bucks for these few pieces of furniture, and that guy still owes me three hundred bucks for fixing his car last week," Dad said. "I need it, but I can wait until the check comes, I don't want you to stress yourself about it Jack." Aunt Joyce replied. "It's not a want; it's definitely a need. So I'll get it for you. You deserve something nice." Dad said, as Aunt Joyce looked up and smiled at him.

Even though I went out of my way to eavesdrop, I still didn't know what the two of those sneaky snakes were talking about. When I went back into the house and tried on the things that I had gotten from mom's pile of goodies, Levi crossed my mind. I wondered what he was doing. After I heard the front door open again, I also heard keys jingle. Without even looking down the stairs, I heard the Suburban rumble and Aunt Joyce's hunk of junk sputtered a sound that I swear I heard on a cartoon before.

When I went back downstairs, I saw the boys grabbing their coats off of the coat rack and heading out the door. "Where are you guys going?" I asked as Larry zipped up his coat. "I don't know; Uncle Jack told us to put on our coats and come on, so that's what we're doing," Larry answered, as he slammed the front door shut. As I peeked out of the window, I saw Larry get in the Suburban with dad, the rest of the boys got into Aunt Joyce's car.

"I wonder where they're going," I said, as I sat down on the couch. After Trudy sipped the last bit of milk out of the bowl, she said, "What do you think you're doing?" "I'm about to call Levi," I said as I reached for the phone. When Trudy slapped my hand, I jerked it away from the phone and rubbed the back of it. "Hey, I already got slapped one time today," I said, jokingly, as Trudy picked up the phone and put it back down quickly. "What in the hell got into you this morning? I thought Uncle Jack was going to kill you." "I don't know, I just snapped," I replied, as I sat there with my arms folded across my chest.

"Are you about to call Edwin the slime ball?" I asked. "You better believe it," Trudy answered, as she smiled like a Cheshire cat. "Well, what in the hell am I supposed to do then?" "I don't know, go plunder in Uncle Jack's room, I think they left the door unlocked." "Really?" I said as I ran up the stairs.

The room door was unlocked, just like Trudy said. As I walked in I noticed how much bigger the room looked without mom's dresser and trunk at the foot of the bed. After checking the bathroom out, I didn't find anything interesting. The next place I looked was in the drawer of the nightstand. As soon as I opened the drawer, I saw condoms, lots of them. After rummaging around in the drawer for a few more minutes I found some Polaroid pictures of a woman dressed in see through lingerie. The pictures were taken from the neck down and the background looked to be at a hotel.

I wondered if this was the lady whose number Trudy and I found in the drawer the other week. As I looked at the picture more carefully I saw that the lady had a small tattoo. I couldn't make out what it said, but it was on her left thigh. After looking at the pictures again, I shook my head and put everything back like I had found it in the drawer. As I was about to leave the room, something told me to look under the mattress.

I followed my mind and lifted the mattress to find a folder filled with papers. As I quickly read the first paper, I saw that it was an insurance policy. The dollar amount was for $150,000. My eyes hadn't seen that many zeros since, I helped Rickey with his zero times tables. I couldn't believe that dad was going to get that much money. I bet this is the check that they are waiting for the mailman to bring. As I looked through the rest of the papers, I found another insurance policy. On this one the beneficiary was Aunt Joyce, and it was for 50,000.

As much as I wanted to stay and look through the rest of the papers, I couldn't. I had to get downstairs and tell Trudy about the important papers that I found. After I put the papers and the mattress back exactly like they were, I ran to the door only to be startled by Trudy coming into the room. I almost pissed my pants because I thought it was dad. "Girl, you won't believe what I just found under the mattress." I said, to Trudy as I pulled her by the arm towards the bed. "Stop pulling on me, I already know about the three insurance policies, the title to this house, and the title to the Suburban."

"Three insurance policies? I only saw two. How did you know?" I said, as I look confused as ever. "While you went outside to eavesdrop earlier today, I was up here being nosy. Oh, I know about the condoms and the pictures in the nightstand too. And, the tattoo on the woman's thigh is the name Rochelle" Trudy confessed, with a smirk. I couldn't believe that she sent me up here to plunder and she already knew all of the juicy information. I could have strangled her, but if I did that- who would I pick up these bad habits from.

After we left the room, we went into Aunt Joyce's room. I went straight to the nightstand by the bed and I didn't find anything. Trudy went to the drawer with the porn and pulled the tape out. "We should watch this." She said. "Eww, gross. I don't want to see that nasty mess." I yelled, as we heard a horn blow outside. Both of us jumped and fumbled with the VCR tape and the old drawer on the dresser. After bumping into each other, we tried to exit Aunt Joyce's room as quickly as possible.

When we got downstairs, I opened the entry door with Trudy on my heels. I saw a black van and thought that someone had turned into the wrong yard, until I saw Aunt Joyce stick her head out the window. "Mom, is that your van?" Trudy asked; as we both walked towards the new jet black Dodge Caravan. "Yep, it's brand new; I traded my hunk of junk for it. What do you girls think?" Aunt Joyce said, as she slid the door open so we could see the khaki colored interior of the van. "It's really nice, but can you afford this mom?" Trudy asked, as she looked at me out of the corner of her eye.

"Yes, I can afford it. I'm sure that I will get that job. I got a feeling that the lady is going to call me with good news. Here honey, lock up the van and come back inside, I'm going to cook a huge dinner today." As Aunt Joyce walked into the house, daddy pulled up in the yard. The way the boys jumped out, you would have thought that they were being held captive or something.

As soon as the boys made it into the house, they all headed to the basement. Trudy and I helped get dinner ready. Just as Aunt Joyce was about to call the boys out of the basement for dinner, the phone rang. It was the lady from the nursing home. Aunt Joyce got the job and had to go in and fill out paperwork tomorrow. I don't know who was happier, Aunt Joyce, me, or Trudy. With Aunt Joyce getting the job, that meant, we were going to be able to spend time with Levi and Edwin.

That night after dinner, I called Levi when dad went upstairs to take a shower. After giving him a heads up about being able to come over on Monday, I talked to him for a few more minutes and wished him a good night. After I got ready for bed, Trudy came into my room, and we discussed how we both were going to get out of the house without leaving the boys here by themselves.

As soon as Dad and Aunt Joyce left for work on Monday morning, Trudy and I both would fix breakfast for the boys. Knowing the boys, they were going to go back down to the basement and fart, burp, and dig up their noses until we called them up for lunch. Trudy would visit with Edwin at his grandparent's house until 12:30 or 1:00. By the time she got back, the boys would come upstairs to eat a quick lunch, then go back down to the basement. Then it would be time for me to go over to Levi's. I would chill with him until 4:30, then I would come home and cook. We had it all planned out, or at least, we thought that we did.

10

Keeping Up

By the time Monday morning came, I thought I was going to freak out. I couldn't wait for Aunt Joyce and Dad to get the hell out of the house. When Trudy got up, she kept a low profile and took a shower just after Dad and Aunt Joyce left. Just as I predicted, when the boys were finished eating, they headed back downstairs into the smelly basement. Once I heard *The Magic School Bus* intro playing, I knew that the boys weren't going to come up from the basement anytime soon.

After Trudy learned that the coast was clear, she dashed out of the front door. Her perfume lingered in the living room as I dialed Levis number. I got comfortable on the couch and watched the clock while we talked about everything from the weather to our Christmas list. It seemed like time was dragging.

In the middle of our conversation, I thought about the nasty tapes in Aunt Joyce's drawer. When I couldn't take it any longer, I decided that I would invade Aunt Joyce's privacy and watch one of her videos. As much as I hated to get off the phone with Levi, I did because the curiosity was killing me. Levi didn't want to hang up first, so I counted to three, and we both hung up at the same time. Before I went up the stairs, I made sure that the screen door and entry door was locked. I headed straight to Aunt Joyce's room after I cracked her door and looked around. I went to her dresser drawer and took out one of the VCR tapes. After taking a deep breath, I inserted the tape into the VCR and turned the television on.

When I saw the first scene I squinted my eyes and watched as things got crazier by the second. I couldn't believe that I was watching a nasty video. I watched the video for about twenty minutes or so before I started feeling warm all over. I wanted to watch more, but after I heard movement in the den, I knew that the boys weren't in the basement anymore. Being that I was really into the video, I hated to rewind it and put it back in the drawer; however I couldn't risk getting caught by one of the boys in Aunt Joyce's room. By the time I placed everything back exactly how I found it in Aunt Joyce's room, almost an hour had passed. I didn't realize that I had been in her room for so long.

While my stomach growled, I yelled, "What do you guys want for lunch?" After the boys yelled out four different answers, I quickly went downstairs and made them some beans, franks, and white rice. After the boys filled their bellies, they went back into the basement. I knew that I didn't have a lot of time to get myself together before Trudy got back home, so I left the dishes for her to wash and went back upstairs to get ready.

After taking a shower and playing around in my makeup, I was dressed in a pair of blue stretch leggings and a baby doll top. I looked cute and I smelled just like Trudy did because I helped myself to some of her perfume. After I looked at myself over and over again in the mirror, I heard someone knocking on the front door. As I crept down the stairs, I prayed that the boys didn't hear the knocking. When I opened the door, I let Trudy in. She had a smile on her face that spread from one ear to the other. Without even asking if she had a good time, I knew that she did. It was written all over her face.

I wished that I could be a fly on the wall to see what Trudy and Edwin did when they were alone. I wasn't sure if they did all the things that I saw on the tape today. I guess I would ask Trudy about that later on. Right now, I had to get out of here so I could see Levi. "Alright Kandee, if Levi tries to kiss you with his tongue, make sure you give him tongue back,"

Trudy said as I walked out of the door. I laughed, and replied, "Okay," as I made my way down the steps of the porch.

I didn't realize it was so cold, I had my jacket on, but the wind seemed as if it was blowing right through me. The closer I got to Levi's house, the wind didn't bother me. My heart thumped loudly as I walked into his driveway and up the steps to the side of his house. I only had to knock one time, and he opened the door. He wore gray jogging pants and a navy t-shirt. When I stepped inside, he closed the door and gave me a hug.

Before we made our way through the small kitchen, I looked at the boxes of cereal that were on top of the refrigerator. Froot Loops, Lucky Charms, and Frosted Flakes. Two out of the three were my favorites, Levi and I had so much in common. When I walked into the living room, I didn't expect to see a fireplace but I did. The living room walls were white, with a burgundy colored border running around the top. I looked around at the pictures as he suggested that I have a seat on the couch. I couldn't help, but stare at Levi's baby pictures.

"Aww, you were so cute. Look at you," I said, as Levi sat down beside me. "Were? You don't think I'm cute now?" He asked. "Of course, I think you're cute." I giggled, as I took off my coat and lay it across the arm of the comfy sofa. "So what do you want to watch?" Levi asked, as he got up and looked at a bunch of VCR tapes on a shelf. "It doesn't matter, to tell you the truth; I really want to hold your hand and talk. If that's okay." "That's perfect," replied Levi, as he sat down beside me and took my hand into his.

From there we talked more and the time flew by. After Levi kissed me softly on the lips, I wanted to melt. He was such a gentleman. Even though I wanted to kiss him again, I didn't. I didn't want to be fast and end up doing something that I might regret. After exchanging another kiss and a few hugs by the back door, I was back out in the wind again. Only this time, I wasn't cold at all. The time that Levi and I had just spent together, kept my mind occupied the entire walk home.

When I got back to the house, Trudy opened the door for me and we went up to her room to talk. After she told me what she and Edwin did, I didn't want to hear anymore. I was shocked that Trudy knew so much about sex. She and Edwin had done everything that I saw on the tape in Aunt Joyce's room. When it was time to tell Trudy about my afternoon with Levi, I thought she would fall asleep. "All we did was talk and hold hands. Oh, we did kiss two times," I said, as Trudy looked at me and rolled her eyes. "Kandee, I hope you don't think you can keep Levi by not giving anything up. You've got to let go of that good girl image." After I sat on the edge of her bed and looked confused, Trudy yelled, "Honey you're going to have to drop those drawers if you don't want some other chick to steal your spot." "Well, I never thought of it like that." "Yes, break him off a little something and see how much crazier he is about you then." Trudy responded. "Alright, I'll keep that in mind," I said, as I left her room.

For the rest of the day I was excited and couldn't wait for the sun to set and rise again. After Dad and Aunt Joyce got home, they talked about their day at work while Trudy and I cooked dinner. Aunt Joyce said that she was so tired that she was going to get under the bed. I laughed, as I imagined her with all of those old people at the nursing home. She had to wash them, feed them, and chase after them when they tried to escape. She had a lot of stories to tell and it was only her first day on the job.

Even though Aunt Joyce was tired, she still volunteered to clean the kitchen. I was happy because that meant that I could call Levi and talk to him at least an hour before I got ready for bed. I knew that it wasn't a school night, but I still wanted to get some rest. I was seriously thinking about giving up my goodies to him tomorrow. That's if he wanted them.

***

The next morning after Dad and Aunt Joyce left. Trudy and I did an instant replay of Monday. She left to be with Edwin until about 12:30 and then I left to spend time with Levi. On the way over to Levi's house, I thought about what Trudy told me last night. While the cold breeze blew, I felt warm all over because I couldn't stop thinking about kissing Levi. When I made it to his driveway, I walked to the side door just like yesterday.

After he let me inside, we sat on the couch for a little while and watched Spike Lee's, *Do the Right Thing.* As Levi and I sat so close to one another, I felt his body heat. With the lights off and thoughts of Aunt Joyce's nasty tape playing over and over inside my head, all I wanted to do was the wrong thing. I really wanted to make a move, but I wasn't sure of what to do. After thinking about it for a while, I decided to give it a shot.

"Hey, you never gave me a tour of your house." "I'll show you, but there isn't much to see," replied Levi, as he pulled me up off of the couch by my hand. As we walked down a short hallway, he opened a closed door at the end. "This is my old man's room." When I walked in, I saw an unmade bed, a nightstand littered with a variety of things, a black recliner, and a small television. The walls in the room were white and the carpet was beige. There wasn't a smell in the room; it didn't smell good or bad. I guess that you could say that it smelled like nothing.

When Levi closed the door to his father's room, he took me by the hand to the bathroom and laundry room. Their washer and dryer were in their bathroom, just like ours was. The room smelled of dryer sheets and was a baby blue color. The tub had a sliding glass door and there wasn't a shower curtain. "So this is where you get naked?" I asked, with a giggle. "Yep," replied Levi.

The only two doors in the hallway that were left unexplored was the closet, which contained the water heater and Levi's room. As he opened the door to his room, my eyes went straight to his insane sneaker collection. He had all of his shoes lined up. His shoes took over half of the space in his medium sized room. Unlike the rest of the rooms in the house, the walls in Levi's room were painted a dark gray color. You couldn't really see the paint on the wall because the walls were plastered with posters.

Run DMC, Slick Rick, Big Daddy Kane, Naughty by Nature, Queen Latifah, and MC Lyte are just a few of the posters I saw on the walls. I had never heard of some of the other groups, though. The smell in Levi's room was his personal scent. If I could bottle the smell, I would take it with me so that I would never forget it. Without a doubt, I was in a trance when I sat at the foot of Levi's bed and pressed play on his silver boom box. To my surprise Bobby Brown's, *Roni* filled the air. I laughed because I never imagined that Levi would listen to this kind of music.

"I didn't know that you liked Bobby Brown," I said. "I only listen to this song because it reminds me of you," he replied, as he sat down on the bed beside me. After hearing that, I made my move on Levi. I leaned in and kissed his lips and from there things only got better. As Bobby Brown continued to sing about his Roni, our clothes ended up on the floor. Under the plaid blanket on Levi's bed, we got closer than close, and I felt Levi's skin against mine.

On that chilly December day, I lost my virginity. When it was all over, I lay on his bed and looked around at the posters. I pulled the covers up to my chin because I felt that the eyes of the ladies and gentleman were watching me. While Levi went to wash up, I put one of his pillows over my face and took a long deep breath. After I hugged the pillow, I said, "Levi, this pillow smells like you. Can I take it home with me?" As he entered the room fully dressed, he answered, "I don't care, but don't you think people are going to look at you like you're crazy. Walking down the street with a pillow?" "Oh, I didn't think about that."

He then bent over and kissed me on the cheek, before he sat down at the foot of the bed. "Don't look at me," I said, as I bent down and picked my clothes up off of the floor. As I headed to the bathroom, Levi said, "I already saw you Kandee." "Well, I don't want you to see me again," I said, with a laugh. When I walked into the bathroom, I didn't bother closing the door. I slowly put my clothes back on until I thought about the time. "Hey, what time is it?" I asked, from the bathroom. "Almost 5 o'clock" Levi said. "I better hurry up and get out of here; your dad will be home soon," I replied. "He probably won't be here until a little after 6:00, he had to work in Myrtle Beach today, and it's going to take him at least an hour to get home."

With time winding down, I got dressed and went back into Levi's room. After I gave him a hug, we exchanged over a dozen kisses. Just as I was about to leave, he handed me one of his pillowcases. It was folded up into a small rectangle. "I hope this is good enough." He said, as I took the folded pillowcase out of his hand and put it in my pocket. I was really on top of the world. I couldn't wait to tell Trudy about this.

As soon as I opened the door I saw Trudy sitting on the couch. She was on the phone of course. After I walked over to the couch, I plopped down next to her and motioned for her to hang up. After she covered the mouthpiece of the phone with her hand, she said, "Girl, I'm not hanging up this phone unless you have to tell me that Michael Jackson is outside, or either you gave it up to Levi." "Shh, Edwin or the boys might hear you," I replied. "Oh my God Edwin, I'm going to call you back." Trudy stuttered, as she hung the phone up.

"I want to know everything. No, I need to know everything." Trudy squealed, as we made our way upstairs to my room. After I made sure no one was upstairs, I spilled my guts about my day with Levi. "Trudy, I did it! I made a move on him and it was incredible." I confessed, as I took his pillowcase out of my coat pocket and put it up to my nose. "What the hell is that? Is that his under wear?" Trudy asked, with her face balled up. "No girl, it's his pillowcase. The one that he's been sleeping on for the past week. It smells just like him too." I said, as I fell back on the bed.

"So let me get this straight, you asked for a tour of his house to get into his bedroom. Listened to Bobby Brown while the two of you were doing it, and stole his pillowcase off of his pillow before you left his house." Trudy said as she shook her head. "Kandee you are smooth, that sounds like something a guy would do." "I didn't steal his pillowcase; he gave it to me. I actually wanted his pillow, but he said that I would look crazy walking down the street with a pillow. That's why he only gave me the pillowcase." I replied, as I took my pink pillowcase off of my pillow and slid Levi's gray pillowcase onto my pillow and hugged it.

"I can't believe you guys did it. Did you guys use a condom?" "After quickly replaying the events of what Levi and I did today in his bedroom, I didn't remember seeing a condom at all. "Oh my God. No, Trudy. We didn't use a condom." I said, as I began to freak out. "Kandee, I'm sure you'll be okay. Just don't let it happen again without a condom," she said. "I can't believe that I was so caught up that I forgot to use protection. I have to see when the next time my cycle is going to come on," I said, as I walked towards the small calendar on my homework desk. "The first week in January, that's when it should come on." I said, as I looked at Trudy. "Kandee, you're going to be fine. No one gets pregnant the first time they have sex." "I hope not." I replied, as I looked at the calendar.

***

For the remainder of week, Trudy and I continued to leave the house every day to be with Edwin and Levi. After the first time we had sex, I just couldn't get enough of him. I wanted to be with him every day and I had to talk to him every night before I went to bed. Trudy said that Levi was going to be crazy about me after we had sex and she was right, he wanted one of my pillowcases too. I ended up giving him a white pillowcase because giving him a pink pillowcase would have his dad wondering where in the hell his son got a pink pillowcase from. I didn't want to raise any red flags because I enjoyed the time we spent together and we couldn't let a pink pillowcase end our fun.

With Christmas drawing nearer, I wondered if Levi would get me a gift. I was a little shy to ask, but I did. All Levi said was, it would be something I would love. After I found out that he was getting me something, my mind scrambled with thoughts of what to get him. After consulting with Trudy, I decided to get Levi a few cassette tapes and a *Sony* Walkman. I figured that would be a great gift since he loved music so much and didn't have a Walkman.

***

On Christmas Eve all of the adults had to work, but they got off early. This threw a monkey wrench into the plans that Trudy and I made. I really wanted to spend my usual four hours with Levi, but today that was going to be impossible. After dad left, Trudy gave me the great news. Edwin's grandparents were home and they couldn't go there to have their fun today. But Trudy was still going to go somewhere with Edwin, only she wouldn't be gone as long as usual. Even though Trudy looked bummed about her time being cut short with Edwin, she was still in a good mood because Edwin was taking her out to eat breakfast.

When Trudy left, I cleaned up the kitchen from breakfast and the boys went down into the dungeon. As I put away the food from breakfast, I decided that I would take a few ingredients over to Levi's house to make something special for him. After I got a brown paper bag out of the pantry, I started filling it with all kinds of things. I knew Levi loved my cooking, so I was going to surprise him and cook something at his house.

After talking with Levi on the phone for over an hour, I heard Trudy come in the front door. When I saw her carrying an arm full of bags, I told Levi that I would be over shortly and ended the call. While helping Trudy to her room with the bags, I saw that she had been to the mall. After we got into her room, we closed the door. "What's all of this stuff Trudy?" I asked as I put four bags on the bed. "This is all stuff that Edwin got for me from the mall today," Trudy replied, as she started taking the stuff out of the bags. As she popped the tags I calculated over two hundred bucks worth of merchandise. She had shoes, accessories, and clothes.

As much as I wanted to stay and look at all of the lovely things that Edwin had bought for Trudy, I knew that Levi was waiting for me, and I had to get the hell out of here. "I'll drool over your things later. I'm going to Levi's." "Okay, but you should change out of your pajamas first Kandee." I quickly went to my room, got dressed, and put Levi's gift inside of my coat. After I was ready, I went in the kitchen to grab the bag of ingredients, and I was out the door.

The walk over seemed like it was longer today, maybe it was because I was so anxious; or maybe it was because I was carrying a bag full of groceries. Whatever the case, I was happy to see Levi's brick house. When I made it to the side door, I put the bag on the steps and knocked on the door. When Levi answered the door, he reached down and grabbed the bag. "What's all of this?" He asked as he sat the bag on the kitchen table. "It's a surprise" I said as I took off my jacket. I almost forgot about the Walkman until I unzipped my coat. "Oh here, I hope you like it," I said.

"This is perfect; now I can listen to my tapes without getting on my dad's nerves. He's always fussing at me about having my boom box turned up so loud. Thanks, I really needed this." He said as he gave me a hug and a kiss on the cheek. "Your cheeks are cold. Let's sit in front of the fireplace," Levi suggested. "Sure, but I want to make you something first. Did you eat breakfast yet?" "No, I didn't. Are you going to make me breakfast?" He asked. "Yes. Find us something to watch on television and I'll whip up something for the both of us." I said.

Levi took his Walkman with him when he left the kitchen. After I looked around in the cabinets, I found two frying pans and a mixing bowl. Then I started on breakfast. It only took me twenty minutes to make French toast, lightly dusted with powdered sugar and fluffy cheese eggs. After I had fixed Levi's plate, I took it to him and came back to the kitchen for our glasses of orange juice. While we ate, we watched *Pet Cemetery* and talked about our New Year's resolutions.

After Levi and I washed the dishes and put them away, he took me by the hand and led me to his bedroom. It was pretty dark considering that it was day time. When I looked over at his window, I noticed that there was a blanket hanging over the mini blind. Next, the flame from a candle flickered, caught my attention. "Take your clothes off and lie down on the bed," Levi said, as he closed his bedroom door. I followed his instructions and Levi joined me. As we lay face to face, he wrapped his arms around me and pulled me closer than close. "Kandee, I've fallen in love with you." He whispered. Then he kissed me, and I kissed him back. "Are you telling me that you love me Levi?" I asked, with a smile. "Yes, that's exactly what I'm telling you." After I rolled over on top of him, I looked into his eyes and told him that I was in love with him too.

For the remainder of the time that I was there, we only hugged and snuggled against one another. I enjoyed being next to Levi, but I had to get back home because the adults would be home soon. As much as I hated to say good-bye, I knew it was that time. After I put my shoes back on, Levi blew out the candles and took the blanket down from the window. He then handed me a slender rectangle shaped box. "What's this?" I asked, as I shook the box. "It's your Christmas gift." He said. I opened the lid to find a beautiful gold necklace with a heart charm attached. "It's perfect, and I love it. Thank you so much." I said as I adored the necklace. "Let me put it around your neck." He insisted, as he removed the necklace from the box. When I turned around, I lifted my braids up and he fastened the necklace. After he kissed the nape of my neck, I turned around and hugged him.

I don't know why I was feeling so emotional, but I wanted to cry. I couldn't believe that today had been so perfect. I enjoyed resting in the dark with Levi and I admired my beautiful gift. I couldn't wait to tell Trudy all about my day. On my way out of the kitchen door, I looked back and told Levi that I loved him. "I love you too" he replied, as he shut the screen door.

11

Off to a Bad Start: January 1991

Winter break was over with before I knew it and the New Year was upon us. There were only two days until school started back. I wasn't sure who was having the most sex now. Trudy and I were neck and neck, it seemed. Every time I told her something that Levi and I had done, she had an even crazier story to tell me about her and Edwin.

After the first week of school, the semester changed, and Levi and I didn't have any classes together. I was upset about that, but we did have the same lunch and shared the seat on the bus. Being that we had a new bus route, we got home later than usual, and I didn't have time to talk to Levi on the phone because I had to get dinner started. Trudy didn't ride the bus the first week back to school and only got home a few minutes before dad did each day. She was playing with fire; I thought she had better sense than that. If dad found out that Trudy wasn't riding the bus, he would flip his lid.

Every day after I finished making dinner, I would go up to my room and write Levi a letter. I sure missed going over to his house; I wondered if he could come and see me sometimes. There had to be a way for him to come over. After thinking about it, I quickly dismissed the thought.

With all of my attention focused on Levi, I had forgotten about checking the mail. When I got off of the bus one day and saw a for sale sign posted on our front lawn, I felt sick. The checks must've came, and I didn't intercept them. I felt like crap for the rest of the night. Aunt Joyce made dinner, but I didn't even go downstairs to eat. That night I didn't call Levi, I only held my pillow and breathed in Levi's scent.

I was almost asleep when Trudy came to deliver the bad news. As soon as I heard her say my name I put my pillow over my head and tried to drown her out. "Kandee, I know you can hear me," Trudy said, as she pulled the pillow from off of my head. "Kandee, the checks came. All three of them, Uncle Jack has over $200,000 and he's purchased a big house in Georgia. I overheard Uncle Jack and mom talking in the living room when I was cleaning up the kitchen." "Georgia? You've got to be kidding me. How am I supposed to be Levi's girlfriend, if I move way to Georgia? He'll forget about me and probably have a new girl within a week." I whined as I buried my head in my other pillow.

"It will be okay; you will probably forget about Levi as soon as you see a cutie down there in Georgia. Oh, there's some good news too. The house that we are moving into is brand spanking new. It's so new that builders haven't even finished building it yet. We probably won't move for another six weeks." Trudy said, as she got up off of the bed and left my room. Immediately, my mind began to spin. All I had was six weeks to spend with Levi, and that was going to be it.

***

The next morning, I got up and got dressed. While Trudy made breakfast, I called Levi and talked to him until it was time to eat. I was pretty quiet at the table. While the boys asked dad questions about the new Suburban he was picking up this week, I wondered when dad was going to come clean about all of us being brothers and sisters. His time was winding down, according to the conversation I heard when I was hiding in the bathtub, Dad said "When the time was right," and it looked like the right time was approaching.

With Aunt Joyce spending more and more time in dad's bedroom, I knew that he had to know that Trudy and I knew what was going on. We were big girls and the walls in this house were thin, without eavesdropping I could hear Dad and Aunt Joyce getting it on. The other night I started to knock on dad's bedroom door and ask them to keep it down. They didn't have any shame, the two of them were disgusting. I wondered if grandma and grandpa knew about this. As I got up and put the plate in the sink, I made a mental note to ask Trudy if they knew.

On the bus, I told Levi about my family issues and that we were moving. "That's a lot to have to go through. Do you have to move?" He said as he squeezed my hand. "I'm afraid so, If I move in with my grandparents, I wouldn't be able to go to this school, and it would still be long distance. We're just going to have to write each other. Maybe I can call you once a month or something. I want this to work." "It will be okay, try not to worry. You know that I will always love you," he replied. "Yeah, I know that Levi."

Later that day we had a test in my history class. With everything so crazy at home, I had forgotten to study. After we had finished the test, the teacher wrote an assignment down for us to complete on the board. While I tried to focus on my work, I couldn't. All I could think about was how life was going to be without Levi. I wondered if the bus driver would assign Levi a new person to sit with on the bus. I knew that all of the girls who liked Levi were going to be so happy when they found out that I was leaving. I bet they would start passing him notes in no time.

As I thought about the girls getting fresh with Levi, my blood pressure went up and I snapped my pencil into two pieces. The sound of the pencil cracking in all the silence brought me back to reality and I noticed that the teacher was passing the graded test papers out. Before she handed me my paper, she said, "If your grade is anything less than a "C" return this test with a parent's signature tomorrow." My heart sank into my toes when I saw the big fat "F" in red ink at the top of my paper. This is the last thing I wanted to show dad; I knew he was going to ground me. He already warned me about being on the telephone so much and threatened to take the phone away if I bought any more bad grades home.

After I had thought about signing the test myself, I remembered the poor soul who did that last week and the teacher called home to his parents. That would even get me into more trouble, so I just decided to show it to dad and hoped that he wouldn't take the phone away from me. When the bell rang, I couldn't wait to meet up with Levi. In the cafeteria, he saved me a spot in line and even carried my tray of food.

While we ate I told Levi about my horrible test score and drank some of his sweet tea that he had purchased from the snack line. "What do you think your dad is going to do?" He asked, as he shoved a long French fry into his mouth. "No doubt, he's going to ground me. So we need to figure out how we're going to communicate while I'm grounded." I replied. "We'll think of something; I can't imagine not hearing that sweet voice of yours before I go to sleep." "Don't worry baby, I'm sure that Trudy can help me think of something sneaky. She's the queen of sneaky."

When the bell sounded, everyone made their way to their classes. Levi walked me to my class and kissed me on the cheek before he left. At that moment I realized, that I wanted him and spent the entire fourth block trying to decide how we could get a chance to be close again. We hadn't had sex in a while, and my body yearned for his touch. I was deep in thought when the teacher said something about a pop quiz. As he passed out the test, I thanked God that the questions were true/false. After reading over some of the science terms, I was sure that I made at least a "C", but I was wrong. When he passed the graded papers out, he said the same thing my last period teacher said about getting the paper signed. This time, a "D" was at the top of my paper, right beside the comment, "Parent signature needed."

On the way to the parking lot, Denise waved at me as I stood in line to get on the bus. I looked around the bus parking lot I didn't see Trudy anywhere. I knew that she wasn't going to ride the bus today and that she was somewhere with Edwin. When Levi joined me, I gave him a hug and I forgot all about Trudy. That was until; I got off of the bus.

After playing kissy face with Levi the entire bus ride, I had a huge smile on my face. As I walked down the steps of the bus, it felt like I was floating. I was on a natural high until I walked by the bush that Trudy normally met me at. She wasn't there. "Where in the hell was she?" I thought to myself. Just as I approached the house, I saw Aunt Joyce's van parked in the driveway. "What is Aunt Joyce doing home so early?" I thought some more, as I panicked and walked towards the house slowly.

I debated with myself about going into the house without Trudy, and I realized that I couldn't procrastinate any longer because I had to use the bathroom. My nerves got to me, and my stomach felt like it did the day of mom's funeral. As my stomach bubbled, I walked up the steps. Before I reached for the door knob, I hesitated when I heard yelling. It sounded like Trudy, Aunt Joyce, and the boys. I wondered what could be going on as I quickly entered the front door.

I'd walked in on a full-blown fight. Aunt Joyce was trying to beat Trudy, but Trudy wasn't having it. As they tussled back and forth, I dropped my backpack and ran over to help the boys break the two of them up. "You little sneaky heffa," Aunt Joyce yelled, as she lunged for Trudy's throat. "No," I screamed, as I grabbed Aunt Joyce's hand and pried her fingers from around the torn collar of Trudy's blouse. After Trudy had realized that she was free, she bolted towards the staircase and ran up the stairs.

While she made her getaway, Larry, Rickey, Samuel, Rich, and I pinned Aunt Joyce down on the couch. She yelled obscenities at Trudy until we all heard a door slam upstairs. Then she started yelling at us. "Get off of me. Get the hell off of me." She screamed, as her arm with the belt broke free. She swatted wildly at all of us with the belt and successfully made contact with our arms, backs, and legs. After we all received our fair share of stinging slaps with the belt, we let her go, and she ran wildly up the stairs after Trudy.

I ran a few feet behind Aunt Joyce and wondered what all of this was about. I bet it had something to do with Edwin, I told Trudy he was bad news. While she pounded on Trudy's door, she yelled, "I know you've been skipping school. One of my co-workers told me they saw you at the food court at the mall in the middle of the day, but I didn't believe them.

That's how I busted you, I didn't go to work today, I saw you get off of the bus and get into that ugly car with that boy. You're not smarter than me; I know what you've been up to. Now let me into this room."

While she twisted the doorknob back and forth, she yelled, "You can lock yourself in that room, but you're going to have to come out of there. You aren't gonna stop until you make a name for yourself; you're going to be known as a little whore if you keep on doing things like you're doing. Do you hear me, Trudy?" By now her face was redder than the hot peppers that grew in grandma's garden. I was sure that I was going to see steam come out of her ears soon if she kept on yelling like this.

"Get away from my door," Trudy screamed, as Aunt Joyce bumped the door with her hip. "Open this damn door, you little slut." "You're the whore and the slut. I know about you and Uncle Jack. The whole community is talking about how big of a whore and gold digger you are. What type of woman sleeps with her sister's husband and has kids from him? What type of woman moves in with her sister's husband a week after she's buried? You, that's who. If I'm a slut or a whore, I got it from you."

After Trudy's rant, Aunt Joyce gasped and put her hand up to her chest. She held her chest like Fred Sanford did when he was having one of his many heart attacks. As all of the redness drained from her face, she looked pale as a ghost, as she looked back at the boys and me. "Mom is that true? Is Uncle Jack our dad? Are Kandee, Samuel, and Rickey our brothers and sister?" Larry asked, as his mother walked down the stairs and ignored his question.

As we all stood in complete silence, we heard the jingle of keys and a door slam. "Is she gone?" Trudy asked as she stuck her head out of her bedroom door. "Let me see," I said, as I ran down the stairs quickly and looked out of the front door. "Her van is gone, so I guess the coast is clear," I yelled, as I closed the front door and ran back upstairs. When Trudy came all the way out of her room, her bra strap was showing because of her partially ripped blouse.

"Trudy, is Uncle Jack our dad?" Larry asked again. "Yes, he is Larry. We are all brothers and sisters. You, Rich, Rickey, Samuel, Kandee, and

I." Trudy said as she went back into her room to change her shirt. "Why didn't mom tell us that Uncle Jack was our dad?" Asked Rich. "Rich, I don't know. I think you may be a little too young to understand the seriousness of this situation." Trudy said as she shrugged her shoulders. "I think she was going to tell you, but I think she may have been waiting for the right time," I added.

Meanwhile, the boys jumped up and down and hugged one another. Trudy suggested that they went back down to the basement and promised that we would bake them some cookies in a little while. While the boys made their way through the living room, I heard one of them say, "I can't wait to tell everyone at school tomorrow that we're all brothers." "Dad and Aunt Joyce's secret is going to be out before you know it. Did you hear what one of the boys just said?" I asked, as we went inside Trudy's room and shut the door.

"Yes, I heard him, and I don't care if it gets out. They're going to learn that being trifling doesn't pay." Trudy replied. After taking a deep breath and wondering how all of this would play out at the boy's school tomorrow, I got comfortable on the foot of the bed. "Alright girl what happened?" Trudy took a deep breath before she answered my question. "Edwin and I skipped school today after first period. He wanted to go and chill at his grandparent's house, but I wanted to go to the mall. Like always, I got my way, and we went to the mall. But little did I know, mom was watching me." "Oh no, I can only imagine how this is about to end," I yelled, as I rolled my eyes and had a fit on the bed.

"Will you stop acting crazy and let me finish the story?" She said as she looked at me seriously. "Alright, sorry. Go ahead." "Okay, after Edwin and I ate inside of the food court, I suggested that we see the dollar movie, and he agreed." "Did she catch you in the food court or the movie?" I blurted. "If you interrupt me one more time, I'm not going to finish telling you the story," Trudy replied, with an attitude.

"A little bit of both actually. Mom kept a low profile and followed us into the movies. Considering that it was the middle of the day, not many people were there. So, we didn't have to wait in a long line, and we practically had the viewing room to ourselves, or so I thought we did. While Edwin and I sat in the corner doing things we only did in his car or at his grandparent's house. Mom watched us from a distance. Ten minutes into the movie, she ran up and snatched me out of the seat by my arm. After she had made such a big commotion, the usher came in and turned the lights on to see what was going on. When mom got a good grip on me, she dragged me out of the theater, through the food court, through the parking lot, and to the van. The whole way home she swatted at me with her free hand and talked pure shit. By the time we pulled up in the yard, I had enough of her yapping. Most of all, I was sick and tired of her hitting me, so I pushed her as soon as we got inside of the house. That's when the fight started, and the boys came up from the basement to see what was going on. A few minutes after that you came through the door."

"Oh, my God. Are you serious?" I asked as I sat up on the bed. "Yes, dead serious. I know that mom is upset about all of this. I wonder if she's going to tell Edwin's parents. She kept asking who they were, but I played dumb like I didn't know. I've never been so humiliated in my whole life. The look on Edwin's face was beyond confused and scared, you should have seen him." "That was crazy, but you know Aunt Joyce is going to tell dad. That's if she hasn't already called him at work and told him." "I don't care if Uncle Jack kills me my life is over any way. I know Edwin probably won't even look my way tomorrow at school." Trudy sighed.

"Well, I'm sure that my two failing test grades will direct some of dad's anger towards me," I said. "Honey, those two failing test grades don't have anything on the pile of shit that I got myself into today. If I were you, I wouldn't even say anything about the bad grades. By the time Uncle Jack gets home, he's going to be a ticking time bomb, waiting to explode all over me." Trudy replied.

After I had left, Trudy alone in her room, I called Levi from the phone in the den. While I told him everything that happened, he suggested that I didn't tell my dad about the two failing test grades as well. We talked a bit more, but when the sun started to set, I got off of the phone. I started a quick dinner of spaghetti and pre-made meatballs that were in the freezer.

As the aroma filled the house, the boys came up from the basement and sat down at the table. I called Trudy downstairs to eat, but she never came.

When I started piling spaghetti and meatballs onto my plate, I heard the front door open quickly. "Trudy, get your fast ass down here right now!" Dad shouted. I'd never heard him yell so loud, and I instantly got nervous. After almost dropping the plate of food that I was holding on the floor. I put it down on the table and peeked out of the kitchen.

It was so quiet in the house that you could hear a pin drop. When I heard Trudy's bedroom door squeak open my heart thumped faster and faster, and the boys peeked around the corner behind me. While Aunt Joyce stood beside dad with her arms folded, she looked up the stairs with a grimace on her face. "Sir?" She mumbled as the stairs creaked under her feet. "What in the hell has gotten into you? Why on earth are you trying to fight your mother and being so disrespectful? Is it true that you skipped school today and was making out with a boy at the movies?" Dad asked, all in one breath. When Trudy responded by shrugging her shoulders, I knew that she had messed up.

"You and I both know that your mom raised you better than that young lady. As much as I want to beat your ass right now, I'm not because I might end up killing you in here. Now go back up to your room. I don't want to hear a single solitary peep out of you. I don't want to see you on that phone, and you'd better have your ass on that bus in the mornings and afternoons. If your mother tells me one more thing about you being fast and disrespectful, I will come out to that school and tear your ass up in front of everybody. Do I make myself clear?"

"Yes, Dad. I mean Uncle Jack," Trudy replied. As we all looked onto the massacre that was about to take place, our eyes bulged out of our heads. Dad snatched off his belt so fast that I thought he did a magic trick. He slapped Trudy with the belt upside her head, her arms, back, and her behind. As she screamed, the hairs on the back of my neck stood up. I whispered to the boys, "Go to the table and sit down." They ignored my order and all charged towards dad. Larry jumped on his back; Rickey grabbed one of his arms, and Rich grabbed his other arm. Then Samuel jumped on top of Trudy and tried to protect her, but it didn't work.

"Dad, please stop," I yelled as he swatted at Samuel and Trudy with his only free arm. Aunt Joyce fussed and told us to get out of the way, while she tried to drag me away from Samuel and Trudy. As she pulled me by the arm, I held onto the banister. When she realized that she couldn't handle us and that we were stronger than her, she stepped back and watched him tussle with the boys. "If you all don't move, you're all going to be in big trouble too," Dad shouted while he tried to catch a breath. The boys had worn him out. It didn't take long for him to realize that he was too old to be dealing with this, and he dropped the belt.

Larry then jumped down off of dad's back and grabbed the belt. He then ran into the kitchen and down the stairs into the basement. The rest of us got up off of the floor and slowly walked away like nothing happened. With Aunt Joyce standing by the door in a state of shock, dad looked around and yelled "When I come back to this house, I don't want to see either one of you black fools. Do you hear me? Come on Joyce." He yelled with wild eyes. Then he opened the front door, and they both left.

When I heard the Suburban crank up and roar down the street, I knew that the coast was clear. After I had locked the front door, I knelt down beside Trudy and put my arms around her. "Boys, go get Larry and eat your spaghetti. I'm going to make sure Trudy's alright." "Okay," They said, as they walked towards the kitchen. As Trudy and I headed upstairs to see what kinds of welts and bruises we had on our bodies, she said, "Thanks for sticking up for me." "No problem, that's what sisters are for," I replied.

12

Valentine's Day Disaster

Two weeks after the knock-down, drag out incident dad still wasn't speaking to any of us kids, and he was doing an excellent job of ignoring us. It was a week before Valentine's Day and families were coming by to look at the house. It still hadn't sold, and I was glad. After intercepting the mail, I learned that our new house was ready to move into. Ever since Trudy told me about it, I wondered what it would look like.

When I finally saw the plans I was surprised. The layout was crazy; there were six bedrooms, four bathrooms, and huge den. I couldn't wait to see it in person, but thoughts of Levi left me thinking that my room at our current house was just fine. With thoughts of moving and starting a new school. I wondered how the people at the new school would react when they found out about this whole sister, cousin thing that Trudy and I had going on. I only hoped that things went well after the move because I had already made my mind up that I wasn't going to take any crap from anybody.

On the brighter side of things, I hadn't made any more failing test grades, and neither of my teachers ever found out that I forged dad's signature. Trudy had been riding the bus, and her relationship with Edwin was hanging by a string. After the day at the theater, Edwin was afraid to be around Trudy, and he still thought that Aunt Joyce was going to tell his parents. Being that Edwin and Trudy didn't have any classes together or even the same lunch, they were drifting apart.

The same night of the brawl, dad unplugged the phone in the den and locked it inside of his room. I hated that I couldn't talk to Levi every day after school, but we wrote lots of letters. He even bought me one of his pillowcases to school. He knew exactly how to make me happy; I was so in love with him. After giving Levi our new address, he promised that he would keep in touch and try to call me at least once a month.

***

Three days before Valentine's Day, I overheard dad make reservations at a restaurant in Columbia. I walked in on the end of the conversation, so I assumed that the reservations were for him and Aunt Joyce. From where we lived, Columbia was an hour away. Immediately, the wheels started turning inside of my head. "Maybe Levi could come over that afternoon, with the boys down in the basement, Trudy and I could whisk him up to my room." I thought. I could definitely figure something out. I had to tell Levi first and see if Trudy would agree to help me pull this off.

That same day a couple came by to look at the house. I made sure I stayed in earshot of the conversation the couple had as they walked through our house. They whispered positive things like, "The bathroom is a good size." And "The pink room is perfect for our nursery." I wanted to shout out, "The basement stairs creak, faucets drip continuously, and my mom almost died in this house," but I didn't. The way that dad had beat Trudy the other day made me think twice.

While I pretended to get a drink out of the refrigerator, the couple opened the door to the basement. I hoped that it smelled like a fart fest down in the jungle, but when the couple came back up the basement stairs smiling, I knew that Aunt Joyce had been down there cleaning. As soon as the couple walked back into the living room, I quickly went down the basement stairs and looked around. The beds were made, and the sweet smell of cinnamon potpourri filled the air.

After the couple shook hands with dad and the real estate agent, they got into their minivan and drove away. I stood on top of the staircase and eavesdropped and felt like I had been punched in the stomach when I heard the news. I overheard that the couple was ready to move in as soon as possible because the wife was expecting a set of twins, plus they already had an older child. While dad showed his enthusiasm about getting rid of the house, I felt sick. Whenever the agent suggested to dad that we should start packing, I felt weak and went to lie down on my bed.

I had heard enough for the day. I silently prayed that Aunt Joyce, Trudy, and the boys would be back soon. I knew that I needed to get my plan together about Levi coming over. It was only a matter of time before we moved and I had to lie next to Levi again. As my mind wandered, I fell into a deep sleep. When I heard a rumbling in the hallway, I woke up to find dad climbing the frail ladder to the attic. "Here Kandee, get this box," He said, as he lowered a box down into my arms. "I got it, daddy. What should I do with the box?" "Take it to the garage, we need to be out of here as soon as possible."

As I walked through the house with the box, I noticed that Aunt Joyce had cooked. My stomach growled as entered the garage. When I saw six more boxes sitting by the garbage can, I looked to see if it was any more of mom's belongings. It wasn't; it looked like everything in the boxes were junk, until I saw a pale yellow phone with a cord wrapped around it. My heart fluttered as I grabbed the phone and put it under my shirt. I made my way back to my bedroom without looking suspicious, and put the phone behind a pile of teddy bears.

Later that night, after everyone was asleep, I got the phone from behind my stuffed animals and crept downstairs. When I reached the den, I bent down beside the couch and plugged the cable into the phone jack. After taking a deep breath, I picked up the receiver and heard a dial tone. I quickly dialed Levi's number, and he groggily answered the phone. I was so excited to hear his voice I almost screamed. After I told Levi how I found the phone he laughed and said, "Don't get into trouble with that phone, I don't want you to get whipped liked Trudy did." After I quietly laughed, I started to tell him about the house being sold, but I decided not to.

The next morning I was sleepy as ever. Levi and I stayed on the phone for three hours. As the thought of everyone having cereal for breakfast crossed my mind, I thought of Levi and how he loves the muffins. Considering that these are the last few days that I'm going to be able to spend with him, I decided to make a pan of blueberry muffins. The aroma in the house smelled so good that I almost forgot that we were moving. That was until dad entered the kitchen with a huge box. "Kandee, it sure smells good in here. I can't wait to taste one of those muffins."

When everyone was finished eating, I wrapped up two muffins for Levi and put them into my backpack. As I headed out the door behind Trudy, she said, "Can you believe that we'll be in our house in a few days?" "No, I can't. I'm having mixed feelings about the move." "Things will be alright; I'm sure we'll make lots of new friends, Trudy replied. "I'm not worried about new friends; I'm worried about my relationship with Levi," I said, with a frown. "I know you're going to miss Levi, but I'm sure you'll find someone to fill his shoes when we get to Georgia." "Fill his shoes? I don't think anyone else could do that." I replied as the bus rolled to a stop in front of us.

***

Valentine's Day at school was fun, but I was beyond excited that I was going to be able to spend some time with Levi this evening. Today was supposed to be a day of love and happiness, but Cupid busted my bubble as soon as our bus pulled up to the curve. Trudy and I already had our plan set in motion until we saw a huge moving truck backed up to our front door. My mind scrambled as I wondered why the moving truck was there. We weren't supposed to be leaving until Saturday.

When Trudy and I got inside of the house, we learned that the buyers needed to move in on Friday, which was tomorrow. They were even going to pay extra money if we could have all of our things out by noon tomorrow. After I had heard that news, I felt like I had been punched in the stomach again. "How on earth was Levi going to come over if we had to get all of this stuff packed up?" I wondered.

I felt like having a meltdown. Right here in our almost empty living room. I looked around at the walls with no pictures, and I began to feel empty inside. I was startled when dad blurted, "While your aunt and I are out at dinner, try to get this list of things done." As dad looked around, he called out things that needed to be packed tonight and Aunt Joyce made the list. When she was finished writing, she tore the paper out of a spiral notebook and handed it to Trudy.

"There is a God." I thought, as I looked at Trudy and smiled. With Aunt Joyce and Dad now upstairs, Trudy said, "If we move fast, we can get most of that stuff done before they go to dinner. Then we can call Levi and Edwin over." "Great thinking," I replied, as we tore through the house like two mini cyclones, packing up stuff and putting the boxes onto the moving truck. Trudy was right. We were almost finished with the list of things to do by the time Dad and Aunt Joyce left.

As soon as I saw the van turn the corner, I got the yellow phone from behind my teddy bears and called Levi. Trudy called Edwin too, but she didn't get an answer. After I showered and freshened up, I called Levi, but I didn't get an answer. This meant he was on his way. While I sat there all dolled up, I felt sorry for Trudy. But I told her about how Edwin was from the start. I wished she would have listened to me.

While the boys packed up the stuff in the garage, I looked for Levi out of my bedroom window. When I saw him walking in the backyard, I got butterflies in the pit of my stomach. I quickly ran to tell Trudy that he was here, so she could keep the boys from coming upstairs. When I opened the door for him, I took him by the hand and led him upstairs to my room. After I had shut the door, he took his coat off and gave me a warm hug and a kiss.

"You think you got enough pink in here?" He asked as he sat down on my bed. "A girl, can never have enough pink." "I never have seen so much pink in my life," He confessed, as he slid closer to me. I don't know why

I got nervous; we had been together over a dozen times. Maybe I felt this way because I knew this would be our last time being together. As Levi placed a tender kiss on my lips, I got very emotional and started to cry.

I fell apart before his eyes, and he held me close. He knew why I was crying, and he let me cry a river of tears without telling me to stop. I stopped crying when my head began to pound. I apologized that I was such a crybaby and told Levi about us moving tomorrow. "So you aren't coming to school tomorrow?" He asked. "No, we have to be out of here by noon and the only possible way that can be done, is if we are all here to help. If tonight weren't Valentine's, we probably would have been packed and gone by sunrise," I replied. "Damn, I can't believe that my first love is leaving me," Levi said, as he grabbed my hand and held it.

After talking about the inevitable, I felt a little better knowing that I was his first love. For the remainder of the night, we lay on the bed and held one another. When Trudy brought up a plate of beans and franks with two spoons, we sat up and ate. "You guys probably have another hour or so before Uncle Jack and Mom comes back. I'm going downstairs to watch television." Trudy said, as she walked out of my room and closed the door behind her.

The hour flew by in no time and the time I was dreading was upon us. As Levi prepared to leave, I started to come undone again. "Please just lay with me for a little while longer," I begged. "I'll stay another ten minutes if you promise not to start crying again," He said. "Alright," I agreed, as we both fell back on the bed. I squeezed him tight and closed my eyes while I breathed in his scent.

I woke up when I heard heavy footsteps coming up the stairs, I jumped up and saw that Levi was still in bed. "Shit," I whispered as I froze up. "Levi, wake up. My dad is home." After Levi looked around and remembered that he was at my house, in my bed. He quickly slid behind the back of the bed. As soon as he was safe in between my pink wall and my pink bedspread, the knob on my room door twisted. I closed my eyes and played possum as dad peeked in on me. He didn't say anything, but I knew it was him because I could smell his cologne.

Kandee's Crush

While Aunt Joyce and Dad moved around in the hallway, I listened carefully. When I heard dad's room door close, I knew it was time for us to make our move soon. A few moments passed and I heard water running followed by soft moans. "Levi, you've got to make a run for it, they're both in the shower," I said, with my face pressed in between the wall and the bed. He got up quietly and gave me a hug and kissed me on my forehead. Tears started to fall from my eyes because I knew that this would probably be the last time that I ever saw him.

As we walked quickly but carefully down the stairs, I held his hand until we made it to the back door. After we shared one last hug, Levi said, "I'll love you forever and ever." "I'll love you forever and ever as well, Levi," I replied, as he kissed me one final time and left. After I closed the back door and walked back through the den, I saw Trudy asleep on the couch. I started to wake her up and ask her how she could fall asleep while she was supposed to be my lookout. But I didn't sweat it. Levi didn't get caught in the house, and I got to spend over five hours with him. As I walked up the stairs, I heard Dad and Aunt Joyce going at it. I didn't care anymore, the two of them could have each other and live happily ever after. All I wanted to do was lay in the spot on the bed where Levi had been laying.

***

After the first week in the new house and the new school, I felt miserable. Even though my bedroom in the new house was twice as big as the one, I was used to having, it didn't matter. My room was pink just like my old room was, but it didn't feel like home. Everything smelled new; all I wanted to smell were some familiar scents. The first three nights in the mini mansion, I cried myself to sleep. I missed Levi. and I couldn't stop reading the box of letters that he'd written me over the span of our relationship.

While Trudy pointed out cute guys at school, I instantly compared them to Levi. When I finally received a letter from him, he wrote that he missed sitting on the bus with me and holding hands. When I wrote him back, I told him all about the new house, the new school, and how much I missed him of course. Towards the end of the letter, I confessed that my dad finally came clean about him and Aunt Joyce being lovers. Even though Trudy had spilled the beans last month, dad had never confirmed it. But we knew for sure now.

While the weeks passed by, I wore the necklace that Levi had given me for Christmas. It was tarnished now, but I didn't care. I never took it off. I showered and slept in it. As Levi and I wrote less and less. I thought of him often, but I started looking at other guys. That next day, I found out that Jacob Camden was interested in me. He was a charming, brown skin fellow that wore khakis, button up shirts, and bow ties. I didn't think that he was my type, but I gave him my phone number anyway. Three weeks after we got to know each other, Jacob asked me to be his girlfriend, and I accepted his offer.

With new thoughts of Jacob bombarding my brain, I thought about Levi less and less. I couldn't resist his full lips and ended up dropping my drawers for him the first week we were officially a couple. After doing it that one time, we couldn't get enough of each other and continued to have unprotected sex. With everything moving so fast, I hadn't noticed that I had missed my period and couldn't keep anything on my stomach. Thinking that I had a virus, Aunt Joyce took me to the doctor, only to find out that I was pregnant.

Dad was livid about the pregnancy, but when he saw his grandson for the first time all of his anger melted away. He was proud to be a grandfather now, and he loved Jacob Jr with all of his heart. With everyone chipping in at home with the baby duties, I had it made. I continued to date Jacob and was madly in love with him, even though his family wasn't.

Jacob's family was the type of family that thought they were better that everybody else. They tried to sweep all of their problems under the rug, but my pregnancy was something that they couldn't hide. After Jacob's mom and dad, begged and even tried to bribe me to have an abortion, it put a strain on Jacob's relationship with his family.

One night after our son was born, Jacob got into a fight with his father. Things got so bad that his parents eventually, kicked him out. Since he didn't have anywhere to go, dad converted our basement into an apartment for Jacob and I. Even though, I still had to sleep upstairs at night and Jacob slept in the basement, I ended up pregnant with my second son the very next year.

At times, I couldn't believe that I had two sons and a fiancé, at such a young age. Jacob was a year older than me and joined the military the same week that he graduated from high school. After I graduated, we got married and had a simple wedding in the back yard. Not long after that, we packed up and went to live in military housing. Things were going well until Jacob started drinking and became abusive. One time he gave me a black eye for not having his bath water ready for him when he got home. After confiding in Trudy, she told dad.

I don't know what daddy said to Jacob, but he never put his hands on me again after that. As our boys grew older and started school, Jacob entered into his cheating and lying stage. He wouldn't come home for days and would even give women our home phone number. The disrespect was so unbelievable that I threatened to move back in with my dad. Needless to say, I never did move back in with dad. I only accepted the cheating and continued to be faithful to my husband.

13

It Was All a Dream

When the phone rang, it startled me, and I woke up from my dream of the past. "Hello." I groggily said. "What are you still doing at work this late; shouldn't you be at home with Jacob?" Trudy asked. "Trudy, you wouldn't believe the dream that I just had. It was our childhood, just the way we lived it. Things we did and said, it all seemed like I was back in the 90's all over again. Reliving the loss of mom, starting my period, getting slapped by dad, and losing my virginity. It was all so real. Levi was in the dream too; his lips were so sweet and soft." I announced, as I wiped my eyes and looked around the room. "Girl, you used to love Levi to death, I wonder whatever happened to him."

"I don't know, but I sure wish that I could find him." I said as I let out a huge breath. "If you found him, what are you planning on doing with him? You're a married woman Kandee." "I probably won't be married for much longer." "Why would you say a thing like that for? Did something happen?" Trudy asked as I started to cry. "Yes, that's why I'm here at the restaurant. Some slut bucket called here a couple of hours ago and said that she was pregnant from Jacob. She knew about a lot of our personal business too, so I know that he has to be messing around with her. How else could she know all of our personal information?" I sobbed, into the phone, as Trudy tried to calm me down.

"Come again," Trudy said. She always said that when she thought her ears were deceiving her. "You heard me right. Jacob is a low down dirty scoundrel; he doesn't deserve a good wife like me. Why does he keep cheating on me? Doesn't he know that it makes me feel terrible about myself and ..." That's all that I could get out before Trudy interrupted me, "He'll get what's coming to him real soon. I am sick and tired of him doing you like this. Everything will be alright."

After listening to Trudy rant for a few more minutes, she talked me into going home. When I turned the radio off and gathered my things from my office I thought about the dream I had. It was crazy how I felt like I was young all over again. On the way home, I saw a *Levi Strauss* billboard and thought about Levi. I sure wished that I could see him, I wonder if he was married or had any children. With thoughts of my first love swirling around inside my head, I almost forgot that I had to face my no good husband.

I turned into our driveway and pulled up beside Jacob's silver BMW. As much as I wanted to get out and do the *A-Town Stomp* on the hood of his prized possession, I didn't. I kept my cool just like Trudy had told me to. After I had unlocked the door, I saw candles lined up. They looked like they had previously burned out and the living room was a little smoky. As I made my way toward the back of the house, I walked over red rose petals and heard the sound of snoring before I walked through the bedroom door.

Soft music was playing as I entered the room; slow jams from the early 2000's. I reminisced, as I walked around the bed. My good for nothing husband lay there, sound asleep in a silk robe. With the front of the robe wide open, I saw all of his goodies. If I wouldn't have received that phone call at work, I probably would have woken him up with a blowjob. The rascal didn't deserve it, though what he did only deserved was a kick in the balls. I shook my head as I watched his toned chest move up and down while he snored. His body was ridiculous, a part of me wanted to pour chocolate syrup on his stomach and lick his abs.

My emotions were running wild, and I felt so confused. I wanted to hurt Jacob one second and make love to him the next. As he continued to sleep, I sat in the chair in the corner and watched him. When thoughts of smothering him came to mind, I quickly undressed and started the shower in our master bathroom. I stepped into the stream of hot water, and I stood there for what seemed to be ten minutes before I squeezed body wash onto my body puff.

As I bathed, I thought about Levi and wondered what he was doing this very minute. Then my mind wandered back to the day I lost my virginity, and I closed my eyes. While the water beat down on my erect nipples, I took a seat on the shower bench and opened my legs. I let out a silent moan as the warm water stimulated my clitoris. While I continued to think of him I spread my legs open a little more and started pleasuring myself with my index finger. "You look like you need some help," Jacob said. Even though he scared the shit out of me I didn't let him know that I was startled.

"Of course, come on in here," I replied, as I gave his thick penis a good squeeze. As Jacob stepped in the shower, he said, "I know you had a busy night at the restaurant. I had a special treat for you, but I fell asleep. Do you forgive me?" While the thought of pushing Jacob down in the shower escaped my mind, I replied, "I forgive you. Now what do you have for me, big daddy?"

Without answering my question he began to kiss me. Then he wrapped his strong arms around me. We kissed long and hard until his penis stabbed me in the navel. After seeing that he was ready to play I massaged his manhood, and got down on my knees. With the water raining down on us I slowly began to lick and suck on him. After I got into a good rhythm, I softly massaged his testicles. Jacob then leaned against the wall and tilted his head back in pure ecstasy and in no time he released his contents into my mouth.

Without turning the shower off, we made our way to the bed. As I lay down on my back, Jacob left a trail of kisses from my neck down to my pleasure zone. He French kissed my lady parts, and I began to shake and shiver. After my first climax I begged him to stop, but he didn't. He kept going and buried his face deeper in between my thighs. I lost my mind over and over again, and just when I thought Jacob was finished, he climbed on top of me.

He entered me slowly and slipped in and out of my wetness. I moaned and gripped his tight butt cheeks, as I enjoyed each and every inch of his erection. He talked dirty while I pulled him closer and grinded up against him. After a few more pumps he exploded inside of me. Just as a drop of sweat fell from his brow, he rolled off of me and fanned himself with a pillow. I waited a few minutes and enjoyed the breeze from the pillow before I got up and wiped off at the sink. I thought about telling Jacob about the call I had gotten from Erica, but decided to wait until in the morning.

When I came out of the bathroom, Jacob was fast asleep. His erection had deflated and was now the size of a small cucumber. I bent down and kissed him on the cheek, and he didn't budge. I then slipped on some panties and a long robe and I went out to the garage to plunder through some of my old things. After moving a few cardboard boxes around, I saw the box that I was looking for. It was marked "Rita's stuff," in bold black ink.

Before I sat down on the cold garage floor, I pulled one of my son's sleeping bags out of the storage bin marked "Camping Stuff." Then I unzipped the bag and I spread it out in the corner of the garage. I sat in Indian style and moved a few things around until I found the tattered *Reebok* shoe box that I was looking for. As soon as I touched the box, my heartbeat quickened, and I felt warm all over. I knew that I was about to open a can of worms if I read any of these letters but I couldn't resist. The dream that I had in my office made me yearn for a taste of Levi; I had to read at least one of his letters.

Upon removing the lid off of the shoe box, I felt butterflies in the pit of my stomach. When I reached inside to retrieve an old love letter, something else grabbed my attention. Even though there were, at least, fifty letters I focused on a plastic *Ziploc* bag that was buried at the bottom. Honestly, I didn't remember putting anything but letters in the box, but that was twenty years ago. I may have put it in the box and forgot about it. Instead of spending another second wondering about what was in the bag and where it came from, I pulled it out and opened it.

Just as I unsnapped the bag, I remembered what it was. My hands shook as I removed the folded fabric and held it up to my nostrils. Levi's pillowcase still smelled like him, and I couldn't believe it. I couldn't believe that I had a piece of him all of this time and didn't even realize it. I had to find out where Levi was, and I was going to need Trudy to help me find him.

After I read all of the letters. I smelled the pillowcase, one more time and put it back into the bag. When I put the sleeping bag back into the camping bin, I put the shoe box back into the box that it came out of and placed it on the shelf. On my way back into the house I took a deep breath and went to bed with Levi heavy on my mind.

While I tossed and turned I wondered if he was married, had kids, or if he was even alive. If he was alive, I hoped that he liked his women with a little meat on their bones because I wasn't a size five anymore. I gained over forty pounds with my last pregnancy, and I still hadn't dropped the weight yet. Considering that my last pregnancy was eighteen years ago, I knew that the weight wasn't going anywhere if it had stuck around this long. I wore the weight well, though I had to admit. My stomach was a little pudgy, and I only had a few stretch marks. In the middle of wondering about Levi, Erica Sumpter crossed my mind. I didn't know how I was going to bring this up to Jacob tomorrow.

After the good loving that Jacob and I had tonight, I actually thought twice about leaving him. I can't recall a time that sex had been this good between us. He hadn't pleased me like this in years. I wondered if he had a clue that he was busted. That would explain the candles and soft music. That was outside of Jacob's character; I figured he had to know that Erica and I had talked.

***

When I woke up the next morning and looked around the bedroom. The room was clean, and I was in bed alone. I yelled out for Jacob, but he never answered. When I rolled over, I saw that there was a piece of paper on top of his pillow. After I sat up, I grabbed the paper, unfolded it, and begin reading.

Kandee-

I'll always have love for you, but you and I both know that this marriage has been over for years. I would like to commend you on your skills in the shower. Other than what happened between us last night, I've lost interest in our relationship. Since the boys are both adults now, I think that this would be the perfect time for us to get a divorce. After speaking with the future Mrs. Camden this morning, she told me that she spoke with you last night. I am finally ready to admit that I have been having an affair with Erica for the last two years. She makes me feel like a king in a castle. Not only that, she has an amazing body, and you let yourself go years ago. I think that you may be able to find someone half as good as me if you lose some of that weight. Please don't call me crying about getting back together, I've made up my mind, and I finally realized that I am in love with Erica, and I want to make a life with her and our new baby. I hope you understand. All I want to do is be happy, and I'm ready to live happily ever after with Erica. You can have the house; I'm sending a moving company to get my pool table, motorcycle, riding lawn mower, 50-inch flat screen, and my clothes. No hard feelings, Kandee. I'm sure that we can be cordial about this divorce. I'll let you tell the boys about this too. I'm sure they'll understand.

Your soon to be ex-husband,
Jacob

"What the…" I said as I reached for the phone. After dialing Jacob's number, I waited patiently for the phone to ring, but it never did. "This number has been changed to a non-published number, if you feel you've dialed this number in error, please hang up and try your call again." I slammed the phone down so hard that the receiver broke. My whole body went into a state of shock, and I had a full blown panic attack.

I thought that I was going to die. I couldn't breathe, and my chest felt extremely tight. While my heart felt like it was jumping around in my chest, I felt nauseated and dizzy. My entire body felt feverish and beads of sweat broke out all over my body. I thought about calling 911, but I didn't. I figured that if I stripped and jumped into a cold shower, I would feel a little better. After I had got out of the shower, I felt a little better, but I needed my big sister's shoulder to cry on. As soon as I called Trudy and she heard my voice, she rushed right over.

***

"Girl, I can't believe that Jacob did you like this, let me read that damn letter again." "Me either, after he cheated the last time, he swore on his grandma's grave that he would never do it again. I knew I should have left him then; he's no good." I replied as tears dripped steadily down my cheeks. "So, who is this Erica chick anyway? I wonder if she has a profile on Faceplace." Trudy replied. "All I know is that she's going to drop her load sometime next month and that she's going to be the future Mrs. Camden," I said as I wiped my eyes a feeling of pure rage came over me.

That was it I was sick and tired of crying over Jacob and I was going to do something about it. When I got up from off of the couch, I told Trudy to come on. As we headed towards my bedroom, my breathing grew more intense. After I crossed the threshold, I ran into the closet and snatched Jacob's designer blazers, trousers, gym clothes, and expensive button up shirts off of the wooden hangers. While Trudy stood there with her mouth open, I ripped more clothes off of the hangers and even emptied his drawers of ties and underwear.

"Help me take this shit to the garage and grab the bleach on your way out of the house," I shouted. After four trips in and out of the house Trudy met me in the garage with a container of bleach. With the clothes in one big heap, I twisted the top off of the container of bleach and walked slowly around the perimeter of the clothes. Then I poured the bleach onto the pile, making sure that each piece was saturated with bleach.

Trudy put her hand over her nose because the bleach scent was so strong. "Don't use the whole bottle Kandee." "Oh that's right, I need to save some for the laundry or possibly for something else," I replied, as I stopped pouring the bleach from the container. "What do you think that I should do with the rest of the bleach?" I asked. "I guess you could bleach the pool table."

After I had bleached the words "Son of a Bitch" on the green surface area of the pool table, Trudy and I went into the house and got Jacob's 50-inch flat screen and a bag of sugar. While I poured the sugar into the gas tank of Jacob's lawn mower and motorcycle, I thought about what I could do to the flat screen. "You could bust the screen out of it," Trudy suggested. "Nah, I know exactly what I'm going to do," I said, as I got a rusty pair of scissors out of Jacobs tool cabinet. When I walked over to the television, I grabbed the cord and cut it into two pieces. "I'd like to see the two of them try to watch this." I hissed.

After destroying Jacob's list of wants, I felt a little better. Trudy suggested that I leave the garage door open, so it wouldn't smell like bleach tomorrow. I agreed, as I put the scissors back into the tool cabinet. "So what are you going to do now? Do you want me to set up a Faceplace account for you?" Asked Trudy. "I don't know; maybe we should have some drinks first and figure out how I'm going to tell the boys about this." I replied as we made our way back into the house.

***

The next day I felt lonely. I wasn't used to being home alone, so I called Trudy and asked her to come over again. She said that she couldn't at the moment because she had a hot date with Mr. Tall, dark, and handsome. After we got off of the phone, I flipped the channels back and forth on the television. I soon realized nothing was on, only reality shows and I hated them with a passion. Even though the shows were supposed to be based on real life situations, some of the crap was scripted.

I figured I would try to set up a Faceplace account without Trudy's help; maybe I could find Levi. After I set my account up, I found Trudy and sent her a friend request. I then got out my yearbook from middle school and searched for all of my classmates. Some people looked the same; some people looked worn out, overweight, underweight, or just plain terrible. I had no luck finding Levi; I guess Faceplace wasn't his thing. Just as I was about to log out of my account, my old friend Denise came to mind.

As soon as I typed in her name, her face popped up, and she still looked the same. After I sent her a friend request, I figured out how to send her a private message that included my phone number. Before I logged off of Faceplace, my curiosity got the best of me, and I searched for "Erica Sumpter." Seven profiles popped up, and I clicked on each and every one of them. Two of the Erica's were white, four were black, and one of the Erica Sumpter profiles didn't have a picture.

After I browsed through all of the profiles, I found out that two of them were pregnant. One of the women was white, and one was black. After going through their profiles, I saw the white Erica with an older looking black guy. As I took a closer look at the picture, I saw that the man wasn't Jacob. Then I let out a breath and clicked on the other Erica's profile. After seeing only one pic of her with a big pregnant belly, I went through the rest of her pictures. There weren't any men in the pictures, but she did have a picture that looked like she was sitting on the stool in my kitchen.

As I looked through more of her pictures, I saw one of her standing in front of a BMW. The BMW looked just like Jacob's and it even had a Dallas Cowboy license plate on the front. "This had to be her," I said to myself as a chill ran up my spine. I was so mad I wanted to punch the screen on the computer, but the phone ringing sidetracked me.

"Hello." I answered. The voice on the other end said, "Kandee, oh my goodness. How are you? This is Denise." "Denise, it's so good to hear your voice. My goodness, it's been a long time. I am doing well. How are you?" After talking to Denise for over two hours, we caught up. She didn't have any kids and wasn't married. She owned a photography business in the heart of Los Angeles. After she had purchased the studio with her life savings, she converted the top level into a studio apartment and used the bottom half as a workspace.

"Wherever I go, I always take my camera with me. That's how I make my easy money." She confessed. "That sounds interesting. I bet you bump into famous people all of the time." "Yes, I do. One day I was having a salad at this restaurant downtown L.A., and I spotted a familiar face. Lo and behold, it was pop singer Roxxi Redd. Not only was she sucking face with a chick wearing ripped jeans and a pair of Chuck Taylor's, but she had a gigantic steak on her plate, and she's well known for being a vegan." Denise chatted. "For real, I think I remember hearing something about that on the radio. So what happened after you spotted her?" "I dropped my fork and snapped twelve pictures in no time. Later that day, I called several gossip magazines and told them about the pictures. That very next day, I was offered $10,000 for the pictures. Without a doubt, I sold them and started stalking celebrities on the weekends." She added, with a laugh. "That's a pretty good hustle." I admitted as I listened to more of Denise's stories.

After we were done talking about her, we reminisced about the good old days. Then we talked about me and everything that had been going on in my life. I felt her sympathy through the phone, as I told her about my cheating husband. "I'm sure things will get better." She said as I heard the doorbell ring. "Hey Denise, can I call you back? Someone is at my door." "Sure, call me anytime, my number is…" As I scribbled down Denise's phone number, the doorbell rang again.

"I'm coming, I'm coming" I yelled, as I ran to the door and peeked out of the peep hole. I didn't know who the man was, but he was very handsome and dressed in blue coveralls. After I licked my lips, I opened the door and said. "You must be here for Jacob's things." "Yes, I am." The handsome guy answered. After I looked him up and down, he looked me up and down too. For a second, I lost my train of thought. "Umm, the things are in the garage, the door is open. I will be out in just a few minutes to show you what you're going to load into the moving truck" I said, with a big grin. "Okay, we'll wait in the truck until you come out."

I quickly ran to my bathroom and dolled myself up, changed my shirt and ran into the kitchen. After retrieving a box of garbage bags from under the kitchen sink, I then ran out to the garage and bagged up Jacob's bleached belongings. When I was finished, I got the cover that belonged on the custom pool table and covered the table with it. I didn't want the handsome mover to think that I was some crazy bitch who got upset and bleached all of her husband's belongings.

"You can come and get the things now." I said as I walked on the sidewalk towards the front of the house. "Okay, let me pull the truck around." The handsome guy said. I watched him as he checked his mirrors and backed the truck up into the driveway. After the moving truck was backed all the way up to the garage, I remembered that Jacob had a few boxes of clothes in the attic. I thought about keeping them here so I could drench them in bleach later, but I decided to ask Mr. Handsome if he could help me get them out of the attic.

"Is this all of the stuff were going to be loading on the truck ma'am?" The short and dumpy mover asked, as he pointed at Jacob's things. "No. I have a few boxes in the attic that I need to get down. Can one of you guys help me with that?" "No, it's against our regulations. We can only load things that are up an actual staircase, not those thin attic ladders." Answered the short and dumpy mover. "Okay, I guess I will have to get them down myself." I replied as I rolled my eyes.

"I can get the boxes for you. It would be my pleasure." Said Mr. Handsome. "No, that's all right. I don't want you to get into any trouble with the boss or anything." I replied. "I am the boss." He responded, as he extended his hand and introduced himself. "I'm Daniel. I'm the owner of Movers R' Us." When I took his hand in mine, it felt smooth and soft. I wondered how he kept his hands so soft, considering that he moved boxes and furniture all day.

"It's nice to meet you, Daniel. I'm Kandee." "The boxes are right up that ladder in the attic. I'll go up first and show you which boxes need to come down." "Okay, I'll be right behind you." He replied as I started climbing the thin aluminum stairs. When I looked back, I saw that Daniel and his employee were admiring my backside.

In the attic I pointed out four boxes of Jacob's things and an air hockey table that had been in the box since I bought it two years ago. Daniel had no problem lowering the boxes down to the other mover and in no time they were finished. After the short and dumpy worker closed the back of the truck, he got in on the passenger side of the truck and shut the door.

As Daniel flipped through a few pages of papers on his clipboard, I broke the silence. "Thanks for helping me get that stuff down from the attic. I know you didn't have to do that." "It was no problem at all. I couldn't turn down a fine sister like yourself." He said, as he ripped a piece of yellow paper off of the clipboard and handed it to me. Without even looking at the paper, I folded it up and stuffed it into my back pocket. Before he walked away, he reached into his pocket and pulled a business card out. After he scribbled something down on the back of it, he handed it to me and said, "If you need help moving anything else around here, don't hesitate to give me a call."

14

Believe It or Not

After the movers hauled away Jacob's belongings, I went through a few things in the attic and the garage. When there was a pile of junk in the middle of the floor, I wondered how I was going to gather all of the crap by the curve with the trash bins. I looked around the garage and spotted Jacob's green wheelbarrow. That was how I was going to get this mess out of here. After filling the wheel barrow up three times, I was finished in the garage.

As soon as I walked into the house, I remembered the card that Daniel had given me. After I pulled it out of my back pocket, I read the words that were scribbled on the back, "Call me anytime." I smiled as I turned the card over and saw that only his first name and the company information were on the front of the card. I wanted to look him up on Faceplace, but I didn't know what his last name was. As I thought about giving Daniel a call later, my mind fell back on Levi.

Since I didn't have anything else to do, I decided to pull out the box of Levi's letters again. Only this time, I bought the box of letters in the house. After I spread the old letters all over the glass coffee table, I took my sweet time and read them all over again. Just when I was about to take Levi's pillowcase out of the bag, I heard the doorbell chime. Since I didn't know who was at the door, I quickly put all of the letters back into the old shoe box and put the lid on top.

"I'm coming" I yelled, as I made my way to the foyer. Through the window of the door, I could see that Daniel was back. When I opened the door, he was standing there with his clipboard and dolly that held the box that the air hockey table was in. "Hey Kandee, sorry to bother you, but Mr. Camden instructed me to bring this box back to you. He said that he didn't want it." Daniel explained. "Well, I don't want it either. You can have it, I guess. Or you can give it away, sell it, or toss it." I replied as the phone rang. "Are you sure? This thing had to cost a pretty penny."

"Excuse me, Daniel, I better answer this call. You know what, just bring it in," I instructed, as I quickly ran to the phone. "Hello," I answered. "Kandee, what in the hell did you do to my stuff? My clothes, television, and my pool table are ruined!" Screamed Jacob. Forgetting that Daniel was here, I yelled back into the phone, "You better be glad, that's all I did." "What in the hell am I supposed to wear to work in the morning? All of my winter clothes are ruined. You did me dirty; I can't believe you would do something stupid. You are so childish." He whined. "Childish, I may be a lot of things but childish is definitely not one of them. Childish is leaving your wife of 15 years with a letter telling her that you're leaving her for a homewrecker. I did you dirty? Did I hear you utter those words? Let me tell you one thing you piece of shit. You better be glad that all I did was ruin your material things. Since you and Erica are so hot for each other, maybe you should just wear your summer clothes to work and cool off, Mr. Hot Stuff."

I was so mad with Jacob that my head was spinning. I continued to cuss after I hung up on him and threw the phone across the room. "Maybe I should come back tomorrow." Daniel suggested as he headed for the entry door. I couldn't believe that I had forgotten that Daniel was here. Jacob had my mind gone. "Oh my goodness." I said, with a look of shame on my face. "I forgot that you were here just that fast. I'm sorry that you had to see me act that way. Please don't go." I said, as I sat down on the couch and cupped my hands over my face.

"Come on Kandee. Don't cry. You'll get through whatever is going on between the two of you. No disrespect intended, but your husband is a real jerk. I overheard him saying some pretty mean things about you when we delivered his stuff a little while ago." As Daniel sat there and talked, I focused on his lips. They were so full and pink. In a way, they reminded me of Levi's lips. I wondered if they were as soft as Levi's lips. I don't know what came over me, but I leaned over and kissed him right on the lips, as he was in mid-sentence.

He passionately kissed me back as I leaned all of my weight against him. We were really into it until the cordless phone rang again. I ignored the phone, but Daniel suggested that I answer it. After I smiled at him I got up and walked towards the phone on the floor. While I pressed the button to answer the call, I kept my hungry eyes on him. "Hello," I muttered. "Hey Mom, How's it going?" Jr said. "Oh, hi baby. Things are going. I need to talk to you and your brother about something important. Do you think the both of you will be available for a conversation on three-way in about an hour or so?" I asked. "I know I will be. I'll call Jr right now and see if he will be able to join us. Mom is everything okay? You aren't sick are you?" He asked with worry thick in his voice. "No, baby boy, I'm not sick. I promise. I will explain everything. Now call me back in an hour and don't worry." "Alright, mom. I Love you," He said. "I Love you too." I responded before I hung up the phone.

I cleared my throat, as I sat back down on the couch beside Daniel. "I'm so sorry for being forward. I've never kissed any man other than my husband, during our marriage. Please forgive me." I apologized, as I looked down at the floor. "I know that you're emotional, considering what you and your husband are going through. I think it would be best if I leave, but if you feel like talking later, call the number on the back of the card I gave you earlier." He then smiled, as he got up. "What about the air hockey table? Did you want to take it with you? You can have it as long as you take it with you now." I replied as I handed him his clipboard off of the coffee table. "I'll take it, but only if you promise to come over and play a game with me one night after I set it up." He said, as he doubled back and put the air hockey box on his dolly. "Sounds like a deal."

I replied as I stood with the door open so he could leave. Daniel nodded his head and grinned as he walked by me.

After Daniel left, I poured a glass of wine and got out a pad and pen. As I sipped the sweet liquid, my body felt warm. I felt myself slowly unwinding, and I began to write down what I would say to my boys. How would I tell them that their father and I were getting a divorce? Even though the boys are adults, I knew that this could possibly upset them. After I drank another glass of wine and jotted more conversation starters down on the paper, the phone rang again.

When I looked at the clock and saw that an hour had passed, I knew that it was my boys calling on three-way. I immediately dropped my pen and finished my second glass of wine before I answered. "Hello." I said. "What's up ma? You okay?" My oldest son Jr asked. "I told him you said that you weren't sick," chimed in Ty. "Boys, I'm not sick." I confirmed. "Well, what's wrong then?" They both asked in unison. "Boys, your father and I are going to be getting a divorce." I responded after I took a deep breath. "Mom, I hope you don't take this the wrong way, but I'm glad that you're finally leaving him. You deserve much better." Jr added. "Well, I'm not leaving him. He's leaving me. It's a rather complicated story, and I don't want to get into all of the technicalities." "Well, you don't need him. I wish you would have asked for a divorce before he did" replied Ty.

As I listened to my boys carry on a conversation about my marriage, I couldn't believe that I had put up with so much of Jacobs crap. When your children aren't bothered by you separating and getting a divorce, you know that a lot of lies and wrongdoing have been swept under the rug for way too long. "Are you going to be alright mom? Dad didn't hit you or anything, did he?" Asked Jr, as Ty spoke up. "He better keep his hands to himself, because I'm not little anymore, and I will come to Georgia and put my foot in his behind." "Boys, I am fine. Your dad didn't hit me, but I am really hurt by his actions. He left me for a younger woman. Her name is Erica. Oh, and boys she's pregnant." I tattled, as I yawned. "What? Mama, please tell me that's not true." Ty begged. "Unbelievable."

Jr hissed. "It's true; it's a big mess boys. But your Mama will be okay. I'm just going to take it one day at a time. That's all I can do."

"I'm going to call dad as soon as we get off of the phone and give him a piece of my mind. I really hate him for doing you like this." Jr said. "Well, I can't tell you what to do. You two are both grown, and I know this makes you just as upset as I am about this situation. I love you boys with all of my heart. Now if you don't mind, I'm going to have another glass of wine, take a shower and hit the sack." "I love you mom," said Ty. I love you too ma. Good night." Jr added.

After telling the boys about the divorce, I felt like a weight had been lifted off of my chest. Jr and Ty knew about their father's dirty dog ways, and they both were on my side. In the shower, I wondered if Ty or Jr called Jacob. To tell you the truth, I wish that I could have secretly listened in to those conversations. Another thing that crossed my mind was the comment that Jr made about Jacob hitting me. He was so young then. I didn't know that he'd remembered that. I guess children remember what they want to remember. As I dried off, I could tell that the wine had kicked in, because I stumbled on my way out of the bathroom.

When I was all snuggled in between my sheets, I kicked my legs around in the bed. I've been sharing a bed with Jacob ever since I was 18. It felt good to have the queen size bed to myself. When thoughts of Trudy crossed my mind, I almost called her, but remembering how sweet Daniel's lips tasted earlier. I changed my mind and got Daniel's business card from out of my jeans from earlier. Then I crawled back in the bed with the cordless phone.

Being that it was only a little after nine, I figured that Daniel was wide awake, and I was right. As soon as he answered he told me that he had been thinking about me ever since he left a few hours ago. "I was really worried about you, and I'm glad that you called." He said. Being that the both of us had to work in the morning we only talked for an hour, but he told me a little about himself before we got off of the phone.

He'd never been married, had one daughter that was 19 and in college, lived across town in a subdivision similar to the one I lived in, and he lived alone. Even though he said that he didn't have a girlfriend, I didn't believe him. He seemed to be such a good catch; he had to be involved with someone. After asking Daniel so many questions, I figured that he would have questions to ask about me. But, I was wrong. He was genuinely concerned with my well-being, and I truly appreciated that.

Before we got off of the phone, he wished me a good night and said that he would be in touch with me tomorrow. He seemed to be a breath of fresh air. I can't say that I'm happy about Jacob leaving me, but if he didn't leave and need his possessions moved, I might never have even met Daniel. It's funny how people cross your paths. Maybe Daniel was meant to be in my life. Whatever the case, I was very excited about having someone to talk to other than Trudy.

That night I slept like a baby. When the alarm went off, I jumped out of bed with a new outlook on life. After I showered, I turned on the coffee maker and made a bowl of cream of wheat. Just as I turned the television on, my cell phone buzzed. Daniel had sent me a good morning text. From that moment on I ignored the news and continued to respond to his text messages. "You were the first thing on my mind this morning when I woke up" was what one text read. I smiled so hard that my cheeks hurt. I hadn't felt this way since way back in the day.

For another thirty minutes, I sat at the breakfast bar in my kitchen and smiled at the text messages that Daniel sent me. Just as I thought about how good my morning had been, I heard a knock on the door. The only person that ever came to my house this early was Trudy, so I figured it was her and I was right. As soon as she made her way through the door, she started talking a mile a minute.

"Kandee, you are never going to believe what I saw on Faceplace this morning." She ranted, as soon as she sat down beside me at the bar. "What, I haven't even logged on today. Daniel and I have been texting back and forth all morning. What's going on?" I said as I sipped on my gourmet coffee. "Daniel, who is that? Nevermind, don't answer that question just yet. You can tell me who that is later. Honey child, you're going to have to sit down for this." Trudy spat.

"I am sitting down, crazy! Now, what is it?" I blurted curiously. "Erica and Jacob are engaged." Trudy panted. "What? How in the hell are they engaged and we aren't even divorced yet? We've only been separated for a few days. You've got to be kidding me." I cried. Trudy then sat down in front of my computer. After she had logged onto Faceplace, she pulled up Erica's Faceplace page. "Look, here's the post right here." When I looked at the screen, I saw a post that looked to be about a paragraph long. Instead of reading the post, I looked at the pictures under the post. There were pictures of Jacob down on one knee, pictures of them embracing, and pictures of Erica's engagement ring.

I immediately felt light headed. While Trudy continued to cuss and fuss, I felt my heart harden and grow a layer of ice. "Do you see this shit?" Trudy snapped. "Yeah, I see it. I'm going to print this out. This is evidence" I said, as I clicked the button on the mouse to print the page. "Girl, you are going to get it all, when you go to court. You'll probably even get his fly ass BMW too." Trudy added as she laughed. "How stupid can you get? I can't wait to show this to my lawyer." I said as I snatched the papers off of the printer.

"You know what, I was having a pretty good morning until I saw this shit." "You looked all happy when I came in here. I'm sorry that I rained on your parade, but you needed to know about this." Replied Trudy. "Yes, you're right. Oh, I talked to the boys about the divorce last night, and they were pissed at Jacob." "I can only imagine. I want to hear how that whole conversation went with Jr and Ty, but what I really need to know is who Daniel is."

"He's the owner of the moving company that came to move all of Jacob's crap out of here." I said. "I bet he has lots of muscles since he moves furniture and heavy boxes all day." Trudy replied with a grin. "He looks like he has a nice body, but he was wearing coveralls. I can tell you one thing, though," I said as Trudy sipped a bit of her coffee. "What's that?" "He sure does have some soft lips." I squealed.

"What?" She shrieked after she spit her mouthful of coffee back into her cup. "Girl, he came back over here to bring back an air hockey table.

Jacob said that he didn't want it. While Daniel was here, Jacob called, and we got in a huge fuss over the phone. He was beyond furious when he saw his bleached clothes. I guess you could say that we both cussed each other out, no doubt he got the best of me because I ended up crying. I even threw the phone across the room. That's when Daniel suggested that he leave, but I asked him to stay. After we sat down on the couch, he told me that he overheard Jacob say some pretty mean things about me, when he dropped off the lawn mower, clothes, and other stuff. After that, we talked about a few things, and I couldn't stop focusing on his lips. Before I knew it, I leaned in and kissed him. He kissed me back too, but the phone rang and distracted us."

"Oh, sookie sookie now" Trudy exclaimed, as she walked over and picked her purse up off of the counter. "Oh sookie, is right. Wait until you see him. He is so fine." I confessed. "Well, does he have a Faceplace account? I can look him up real quick." Trudy replied. "He only has a business account and not a personal one. I asked him last night." "So did you give up on finding Levi?" She asked. As I bent down and picked up the worn shoebox that held Levi's letters and old pillowcase, I answered "Hell no!"

***

On the way to work, I tried not to think about Jacob being engaged, but it was impossible. Questions filled my head as I stopped at red lights and stop signs. Could he actually propose to someone else if we were still legally married? Did I really want to sign the papers when it was time? Was I going to change my last name back to Blue? Was I going to have to move? I had no clue, but I knew that I couldn't afford the mortgage on my house by myself and the rest of the bills.

I liked the lifestyle I lived. I drove a Volvo SUV and didn't have a closet full of high dollar clothes, which was perfectly fine with me because I didn't need all of that. Middle-class living was fine with me. I was satisfied with just having the bills paid. Coming home to a decent house, in a decent neighborhood was definitely a blessing. I deserved to be happy, with or without Jacob and that was the bottom line. From that second forward, I decided that I would hang Jacob out to dry. I was going to take it all, the house, his money, and his business. If anyone was going to be living happily ever after, it was going to be me.

The note that Jacob left was only a small piece of the puzzle of my master plan. Over the years of our marriage, I kept a journal of the verbal abuse as well as the phone records from Jacob's cell phone bills. I knew that he was having hour long conversations in the middle of the night and on his lunch breaks. I was going to use all of that evidence against him in court. I couldn't wait to see his face when he found out that I had kept up with his every move.

As the pictures that Trudy had shown me on Erica's Faceplace page came to mind, I could have sworn that I was looking at them. They were embedded in my mind, and I couldn't stop thinking about them. All of a sudden, I wanted to hurt Jacob all over again. Before I got out of my car, I prayed that a lightning bolt would strike him down. Not tomorrow, but today. I quickly took back my prayer of Jacob's demise and asked God to forgive me. I knew that vengeance wasn't mine and that God would deal with Jacob for breaking his vows in due time.

15

Getting to Know You

That same night, Daniel invited me over for a game of air hockey. He'd put the table together and even ordered take-out. After I went home and showered, I slipped on a pair of jeans and a low cut blouse, and I was out the door. On the drive across town, I listened to Bobby Valentino's CD. As I sang along with Anonymous, I noticed a BMW like Jacob's a few cars ahead of me. As curiosity got the best of me, I sped up to see if it was Jacob. It was Jacob's car, but the driver of the car was a woman. I assumed that this was the future Mrs. Erica Camden.

As I pulled up beside her, I looked down into the vehicle and saw her belly. It was huge, and she wasn't wearing a seat belt. I tried to get a better look at her, but I swerved and almost hit a man on a moped. After getting my eyes full, I had to pull into a convenience store parking lot and gather my nerves. When my nerves were back together and my heart rate was normal, I pulled back onto the highway and drove to Daniel's house.

Daniel's neighborhood was real nice. The yards were much bigger than the ones in my neighborhood, but it seemed like every other house looked the same. A few of the houses had different color bricks, or siding, but that was it. When I saw the moving truck parked in front of the garage, I knew that I followed the directions and had made it to Daniel's house. The gray exterior stood out and the rich red bricks that lined the walkway looked expensive. His place definitely had curb appeal. After I parked on the other side of the moving truck, I got out and walked up the sidewalk.

When I rang the doorbell, Daniel came to the door in no time and opened it. "Come in beautiful," He said, as he took my hand and kissed it. "Well hello there handsome." I replied as he took me by the hand and led me through the foyer. I was surprised by the interior of the house, and I absolutely loved the open floor plan. Everything matched, from warm khaki colored walls, to the curtains and the pillows on the couch. There weren't any floral patterns in sight, but that was alright.

As soon as I took my jacket off, Daniel laid it across the back of a leather recliner. "Would you like something to drink?" He offered, as he walked into the kitchen. "Sure. Just a glass of cold water for now." I said as I got comfortable on the couch. "One glass of water coming up. Oh, I didn't order the food yet. I wasn't sure what you wanted from the Chinese restaurant." "Well, I usually order pork fried rice with sweet and sour chicken, but I want to try something different tonight. Just order what you like." I insisted. "Okay, I'll place the order, and then I will give you a tour of my place." He replied as he went back to the kitchen.

My eyes wandered around the living room and looked at the pictures of what I assumed to be his daughter. The other pictures of ladies and older men I assumed to be his sisters, aunts, brothers, cousins, or uncles. Daniel broke my train of thought when he said, "I ordered the food. It should be here within the next twenty minutes. Are you ready for the tour?" "Sure," I replied, as I sat my glass down on a coaster.

"Well, obviously this is the living room, and that's the kitchen." He pointed as we headed up the staircase. "This hall leads to the rest of the house. That's my home office, here's the hall bathroom, next is my daughter's room, and this is my room. When we got back downstairs he showed me the den and we looked out a window that overlooked the back yard. "This is a beautiful house," I said as we walked through the laundry room. "Thank you. Now come check out my man cave, it's in the garage." As we headed to the garage. Daniel turned on the lights and we walked down a few steps into what seemed to be another world.

The garage floor had some kind of laminate flooring on top of the cement. There were, at least six plush recliners all lined up in a row in front of a projection screen. When I saw the full bar, which was complete with a keg, stove, and industrial size refrigerator, I was amazed. "Damn Daniel, this set-up is all that. I bet the guys love hanging out over here." I said as I continued to look around. "Yeah, they do. Sometimes they don't want to go home."

"Do you mind if I have a look behind the bar?" I asked. "Of course not, go ahead. Hey, do you think you might want to watch a movie down here on the big screen?" Daniel asked as the doorbell chimed. "Sure, that sounds fun." "Great, that must be our food." He announced, as he scurried up the steps into the house. After opening the cabinets, I looked in the refrigerator and freezer. Chicken, steaks, sausage, fresh veggies, and even whipping cream were on the shelves along with many other goodies.

"I bought your water in here. I wasn't sure if you wanted it still, but here it is just in case." Said Daniel, as he set my glass and the bag of Chinese food down on the counter. "You like to cook?" I asked as I closed the door to the huge refrigerator. "Oh yeah. I went to school for culinary arts, but after my dad passed away and left me his moving company. I had a change of heart and decided to keep the family business. He'd worked so hard for it; I hated just to let it go down the drain."

"That's really sweet," I said as I sat down beside him at the bar. "I'll do anything to keep a smile on my mother's face." "I can tell that she raised you well. Any other guy would have taken advantage of me the other night when I was upset, but you didn't" I pointed out, as I softly elbowed him in his side. After he smiled, he asked, "Did you decide what kind of movie you wanted to watch?" "No, it really doesn't matter. As long as there's a happy ending."

After we ate, I drank a glass of beer straight from the tap and got cozy in a tattered, but comfortable recliner. As I sat in front of the projection screen he made the announcement that we would be watching "*Norbit*," I had only seen the movie once in the theater, but everyone was laughing and talking so much, I didn't really know what was going on. Within the first thirty minutes of the movie, I had laughed so hard that my side hurt. I didn't know where Eddie Murphy came up with this stuff, but it was hilarious.

When the movie was over, Daniel asked me if I wanted to go back into the house. I declined and told him that the recliner I was sitting in was so comfortable; I didn't want to get up. While we talked, we drank beers and took turns going to the bathroom. The last thing I remembered was discussing football before I fell asleep.

That morning I woke up in the recliner beside Daniel. He was still asleep, so I got up and went to the bathroom. After I washed my face and swished some mouthwash around in my mouth. I headed to the kitchen and prepared breakfast, just like the one's I used to make when I was younger. Being that Daniel loved to cook too, he had all of the ingredients that I needed. I prepared biscuits made from scratch, grits, link sausage, and cheesy eggs.

After the aroma made its way down into the man cave, Daniel woke up and said good morning as he passed by the island in the kitchen. "I should be cooking you breakfast." He said. "You can cook me something later on this evening." I said as I invited myself back over. "It sounds like a date," he confirmed, as he poured us each a glass of orange juice.

When we were finished eating, I cleaned up the mess I'd made in the kitchen. After I asked Daniel what he was cooking for us tonight. He said that it was a surprise and kissed me on the cheek before I left. On the way home I passed by the motorcycle dealership that Jacob purchased his black on black Harley. I remembered how good the wind felt blowing through my hair as took me for a ride on it for the first time.

A smile spread across my face until I immediately thought about how many of Jacob's whores had enjoyed the vibration between their legs on his motorcycle. I rolled my eyes at the thought and I sped up because I had to get showered and dressed for work. When I pulled into my drive way, I quickly got of my car and went inside. After I unlocked the door, the first thing I saw other than the clock on the wall, was the light blinking on the answering machine.

With only twenty minutes to get in and out of the house, I debated on pushing the blinking button on the answering machine. I wanted to have a good day and didn't have time for any bad or negative news. After I washed off, I put on my chef pants and jacket. I grabbed an overnight bag from out of my closet and packed work clothes for tomorrow, two pairs of panties, a pair of bedroom shoes, peach scented body lotion, and a pair of cute satin pajamas. I figured that I would be prepared to stay over at Daniel's house tonight just in case I drank too much. On my way out the door I grabbed my purse and looked at the clock. I had ten minutes to get to work. With the light on the answering machine still blinking, I shut the door and hoped that it wasn't important.

***

After I left work, I looked in the car, but I couldn't find my overnight bag. I could have sworn that put it in the car this morning. With my bag missing, I had to go back home. As I entered the door I saw my overnight bag was right beside the door. I grabbed it and put the strap over my shoulder as I made my way out of the house again. Only this time, I looked over at the flashing light on the answering machine and not the clock. I'd better check it I thought as I walked over and pressed the button on the light as soon as I heard Jacob's voice, I knew that I should have let the stupid light keep blinking.

"What kind of mother encourages their children to call their father and disrespect them? What kind of lies did you fill Ty and Jr's head with? I should have told them about this situation myself; I knew you would screw it up. You can't do anything right with your simple ass. Do me a favor and make sure you sign your name on the right line when you get the separation papers this week you stupid bitch."

I couldn't believe him. I was so mad that I wanted to punch a hole in the wall. I thought about deleting the message, but I decided to save it so

Ty and Jr could listen to it. Jacob had officially flipped his lid, and I hoped he got what he deserved soon. With evil thoughts of things I could do to him floating around inside of my head, I locked up the house and took several deep breaths on the way over to Daniel's house.

When I pulled up into his driveway, I could already smell a mouth-watering aroma outside. I quickly grabbed my overnight bag and purse before I locked my car. The closer I got to the door, my stomach began to growl. I only had to ring the doorbell, once and Daniel came to the door wearing a pair of blue lounge pants, a t-shirt, and an apron that read "Kiss the cook." I greeted him with a kiss and he looked surprised as he took my purse and overnight bag. "Your apron says to kiss the cook." I said as I pointed at it. "Oh, I didn't even notice, but that sure felt nice. "Thanks." I said as I crossed the threshold.

"You look so cute in your checkered chef's pants." He admitted as he sat my things down on the couch. "Thank you. It sure smells good in here." I uttered, as I headed towards the stove. "Where do you think you're going?" He asked as he guarded the entrance with his lean, strong body. I playfully tried to get by him, as he grabbed me by the waist. With us standing face to face, he looked down into my eyes and said, "I'm sorry, but the kitchen is off limits." "You better be glad, I'm too tired to put up a fight." I giggled, as I put my hands up in the air. When he let me go, he went back to the kitchen and stirred something around in the pot. "Hey, would you mind if I freshened up a little? I asked as I grabbed my overnight bag off of the couch. "Of course not, make yourself at home. There are clean towels in the linen closet in the hallway." "Alright, I'll do just that." I confirmed as I walked up the stairs.

After I got a towel and a washcloth out of the linen closet, I went into the bathroom and stripped. Then I sat on the toilet for a few minutes, started the shower, and got in. As the warm water rained down on me, Jacob's message echoed over and over inside of my head. How could he be so ignorant? I thought, as the water washed all of the suds off of my body.

When I was fresh and clean, I turned the shower off and stepped out onto the rug. After I dried off, I rubbed peach lotion all over my body and reached into my overnight bag. I pulled out my panties first and put them on. Next, I dug in the bag for my pajama top and put it on. When I reached in for my pajama bottoms, I didn't find them. My heart dropped, as I emptied the bag and saw that they weren't in there.

"Dinner is ready, Kandee." Daniel said, from the other side of the door. "Okay. I'll be out in a few minutes" I replied as I panicked. "What in the hell am I going to do?" I asked myself, as I came to the conclusion that I had two choices. I could ask Daniel for a pair of his lounge pants, put on my clean work pants, or go out there with just the pajama top and undies on.

Even though it was unlike me, I decided to go out wearing only my pajama top, my undies, and my bedroom shoes. I had beautiful legs and no one had never seen them except for Levi and Jacob. Tonight I was going to add Daniel to that list. After I put all of my things back into my overnight bag, I opened the door to the bathroom and walked out in to the living room.

Before Daniel could see me, I sat down on the couch and covered my thick thighs with one of the pillows that were on the couch. "There you are. Come on, we can eat in the man cave. I've got everything set up." He said, as he turned around. "Alright." I said as, I got up and walked closely behind him. After we walked down the steps, I saw that Daniel had placed as table cloth on top of the small card table.

With the lights low and the candles flickering, I felt extra special and I almost forgot that I didn't have on any pants. When Daniel pulled out the chair for me, he saw my rump roast and thunder thighs. The look on his face was unforgettable. "Damn, I said, that you could make yourself at home, but I didn't know that's how you got down." He blurted, as he stared at my physique. "I guess he liked what he saw because he was all smiles for the rest of our meal.

Daniel cooked smothered chicken thighs with steamed new potatoes and fresh spinach. The dinner was delicious. The only man that had ever cooked for me was my dad and he couldn't cook worth two cents. After we ate, we had a few drinks and sat in the same two recliners that we slept in last night. We talked and I told him about the rude message that Jacob left on my answering machine. I tried to act like my feelings weren't hurt, but Daniel saw that I was about to cry and suggested that he turn the radio on and play a game of air hockey.

I cheered up as he showed me how to play. When he stood behind me and bent my body over the table, I knew that he was getting turned on because there I felt a slight bulge on my behind. After playing a few games Daniel and I had to play a tie breaker. On the last shot, the puck came soaring from Daniel's end of the table and I blocked it, but the puck jumped up and hit my knuckle.

"Ouch", I yelled, as I jumped up and down. "Are you okay?" Daniel asked, as he ran over and grabbed my hand. "Let me see. I don't think that the skin is broken." I hoisted myself onto the air hockey table and Daniel kissed my knuckle. "Is it better now?" He asked as he took a few steps and positioned himself directly in between my legs. "Yeah, I think so." I answered, as he got closer and kissed me dead on the lips.

My head spun as we kissed and kissed. I had forgotten all about my sore knuckle and Jacob's rude message. As we continued to kiss, he nibbled on my neck. All of a sudden it felt like someone had turned the heat on. I came out of my satin pajama top around the same time Alicia Key's, *Un-thinkable* started to play. As the speakers thumped, Daniel took his shirt off, and we were chest to chest. I became even more aroused as I listened to the words of the song.

When he took his tongue and caressed my breast. I felt as if my soul would leave my body. I was on fire, and I was curious about what Daniel was packing, so I let my hands roam. As they made their way down his chest and abs, I stuck one hand into the waistband of his pants and began to stroke his man-meat. As it throbbed in my hand, I slid down off of the table and dropped down to my knees.

I couldn't help myself. I took him into my mouth and hungrily pleased him. As I sucked and stroked his member, Daniel let a few moans escape from his mouth. When I couldn't take it anymore, I stood back up and took off my panties. After he admired me for a few seconds, he kissed me long and hard before he turned me around and bent me over the table. My bare skin went into a state of shock as it made contact with the cold table. My nipples turned rock hard as Daniel held onto my waist as he slid into my folds of wetness. With me pinned against the table like this, I felt like I was about to explode. I didn't know how much more I could take.

I was so excited that I moaned the entire time he pumped his thickness inside me. I gasped, and a gush of wetness spilled down my legs. While I continued to climax, Daniel came undone and collapsed on top of my back. My heart thumped like a drum as my breathing steadied. When he stood up and withdrew himself from me, he slapped me on my ass and said "Damn, that was good. I think I'm in love." "No, I think I'm in love." I said as I wiped the wetness from the inside of my thighs with my pajama top.

16

No She Didn't

My day was off to a great start and I had just opened my eyes. Waking up next to Daniel was like a dream come true. After we made love again, I got up and got ready for work. The drive to work was normal. I went through the same four stoplights and over the downtown bridge as usual. I hadn't heard any more from Jacob since he left the message on my answering machine and cussed me out.

In the midst of thinking about Jacob. I wondered if Erica had posted any more pictures of them on Faceplace. I hadn't logged into my account since Trudy pulled up those pictures the other day. I thought that it would be better if I kept it that way because my urge to know what Erica and Jacob were up to was strong. The feelings and thoughts that I felt inside were pretty terrible. I wanted to choke slam her, and I wasn't sure if I was strong enough to complete that task. I didn't care all I wanted to do was hurt Erica and maybe even Jacob.

At work, I took my anger out on whatever I was chopping on my cutting board. At the moment, I was in the middle of chopping carrots for a salad when I heard my manager say, "Kandee you have a call on line one." Instantly my stomach dropped, and I thought about the last call I had received from Erica at work. Without putting the knife down, I walked to the phone and answered, "Who the hell is this?" "It's me, Trudy. My cousin that works at the hospital just called and said that

Jacob was admitted and that he is on life support." "Life support? Oh my God, I'm on the way right now." I yelled, as I dropped the knife and ran to get my keys.

When I arrived at the hospital, Trudy was already in the waiting room. "Where is he? Where is Jacob?" I asked as I made my way to the lady at the desk in ICU. "Ma'am, please calm down, Jacob Camden's wife has requested that he has no visitors. So we have to abide by her rules. I'm sorry," Said the lady. "Excuse me!" I yelled as Trudy tried to calm me down. "His wife? I'm his wife. I don't know what in the hell Erica Sumpter told you, but she's just his fiancée. I am still legally his wife. I haven't signed any papers yet, and Jacob is still my husband." I broke down into tears because I was so angry.

I couldn't believe that Erica did this. She must've bumped her head if she thought that she was going to get away with this. I guess she heard all of the commotion and walked out into the hallway to see what was going on. When she saw that I was the one making all of the noise, she tried to duck back into Jacob's room before I could see her. "Erica, you better be glad that you're pregnant or else I'd whip your ass." I shouted.

"Ma'am, if you don't calm down, I'm going to have to call the police." A tall white security guard then walked up. "I'm calm," I growled, as I looked across the hall at Erica. "Now will one of you ladies, please tell me what's going on." The officer asked. Before I could say anything Erica said, "I'm Erica, Jacob's fiancée. We're getting married soon." "Okay, you're the fiancée, so who are you?" Asked the security guard. After I took a deep breath, I said, "I am Kandee Camden, Jacob Camden's wife. We are separated, but I haven't signed any divorce papers. So legally, I'm his wife." I then reached into my wallet and pulled out my driver's license and a wallet sized copy of our marriage certificate and handed it to the security guard.

"This looks pretty legit," said the guard, as he looked over in Erica's direction. With the shoe on the other foot, tears began to roll down Erica's face as she headed back into Jacob's room. "What in the hell do you think that you are doing?" Asked Trudy. "I'm going to get my things." Replied Erica, with an attitude. "According to the staff at the desk, his wife doesn't want him to have any visitors. Kandee will bring your things out in a bit, now go and wait in the waiting room or something." Trudy snapped, as she looked at Erica. Erica looked back at the guard and me, and stormed into a nearby ladies room. I knew she was crying. I could hear her sobs from where I was standing.

"Since the imposter is gone. Can somebody please tell me what in the hell is going on with my husband?" I hissed, as I pounded my fist on the counter. "I'm going to call the doctor to come back; he just left a few minutes ago. I am so sorry about the mix-up Mrs. Camden." Said the lady behind the desk. As soon as I turned my back and started talking to Trudy, the lady grabbed the phone and paged the doctor over the intercom. "Mrs. Camden, you can go inside the room now if you'd like. When the doctor comes, I will tell him that you are waiting." "Thank you, I'm sorry for yelling at you earlier." I apologized, as I grabbed Trudy's hand and walked towards Jacob's room.

Before I opened the door, I took a deep breath. I was mad as hell at Jacob for leaving me. However, I wasn't sure if I was ready to see him in such bad shape. All sorts of tubes and cords were coming from his body, and he looked like he was miserable. All of the good memories that Jacob and I shared came rushing back, but they did not last long as all of the bad memories pushed the good ones right back out. With tears in my eyes, I asked Trudy not to leave me alone. Being in this room with Jacob reminded me of the day my mother passed away.

As soon as Trudy sat down in a chair near the hospital bed, the door swung open. Two people dressed in scrubs walked in and approached me. "You must be the real Mrs. Camden," the man said that wore a white long sleeve coat. "I'm Dr. Banujo, and this is our residential doctor, Ms. Inman. I'm sorry about the mix up from earlier. Please forgive us." He said, as we all shook hands. "So what's going on with my husband? What exactly happened to him?" I asked.

"Mr. Camden was in a motorcycle accident where he sustained major head, neck, and back injuries. There is swelling on his brain, and his back is broken in two places. He also broke both of his collarbones. He is on a ventilator, and it doesn't look good. The chances of him waking up from this coma are less than 1%. You should consider calling in the family." Advised Dr. Banujo.

"Is he in any pain?" I asked as tears dripped from the corners of my eyes. "He's not in any pain; I can assure you. If you let him stay hooked up to these machines and he starts showing signs of brain activity, he will never be the same again. He'll be in a vegetative state and will need around the clock care. Since Mr. Camden doesn't have any advanced medical directives, all of the decision making falls on you; considering that you're his wife. Many family members hate to see their loved ones like this, and make the decision to remove them off of life support." "Oh my God, I've got to call my sons." I responded as I felt sick to my stomach.

"Take some time and think about it, pray if you have to. We're going to leave you alone for a while. If you have any more questions, let the nurse at the desk know, and she will page me." Said the doctor as he and the resident doctor shook my hand again before exiting the room. "I'm going to give you some alone time with Jacob; you look like you need to talk to him about something." Trudy said. As I shook my head, I replied "You know me so well. Yes, I definitely have some things that I need to get off of my chest. All I need is twenty minutes." "Okay, I will be right outside of that door," Trudy replied, as she picked up her purse and left me alone with Jacob.

After I wiped my face with the sleeve of my shirt, I whispered, "Jacob, did you know that you were my second love? I bet you had no clue that you were the second man that I had sex with, and I hadn't had sex with any other man since we've been together, until last night. The day that I met you, I never imagined that you would have ever done me like this. You acted like you loved me and cared for me when we were living with my dad, but I think that was all a front. My dad had a soft spot for you, and you paid him back by making his daughter's life miserable. You've beaten me, verbally abused me, cheated on me, and disrespected me throughout our entire marriage. Now your life is in my hands. Can you believe that you son of a bitch?" I hissed, as I slapped the side of Jacob's face.

"That's right. I get to decide whether you stay hooked up to this machine or if you meet your maker. I knew that God would fix you for treating me so badly; I just didn't know that it would happen so soon. All I ever really wanted to know was why. Why did you treat me the way you did? Wasn't I a good wife? I cooked, cleaned, worked, raised our boys, and I had sex with you even when I didn't feel like it. If you can hear my voice and you want to live, blink once or move your finger. I'll take that as an apology for all of the bullshit you've put me through. I'm going to give you an hour to make your move. If you don't move by then, I know that you have no desire to live, and I will tell the doctor to pull the plug."

After I had given Jacob his speech, I sat in the chair that Trudy sat in and watched him like a hawk. He didn't move a muscle. When I remembered that Trudy was outside in the hall, I opened the door and let her in. "Are you okay Kandee?" She asked, as she went and stood beside Jacob's hospital bed. "Yeah, I think so. I need to call the boys, though. Dammit, I should've called them sooner." "It's okay. I called them, and both of them are on their way. Ty caught a flight and Jr is riding the train," She announced. "What would I do without you?" I asked, as I walked over to Trudy and gave her a hug.

After a few had minutes passed, I heard a phone ringing, and it wasn't mine or Trudy's. Trudy and I both looked at Erica's purse and realized that we had forgotten to take it to her. "Let me take this heffa her purse," I said, as I picked the purse up and headed towards the door. "No ma'am, I'll take it to the little slut bucket, as soon as I look through it and see what's in it." Trudy chuckled, as she picked Erica's hobo style purse up and emptied the contents on the foot of Jacob's hospital bed.

"Girl, if you don't take a look at all of this shit," Trudy suggested. "I'm not looking through that woman's purse." I declared as I directed my attention towards the television. "Okay, you don't have to look because; I'm going to tell you every little thing she has in here. Starting with this pack of *Juicy Fruit*." "Okay, okay. I'll look through the stuff with you." I snapped, as I stood on the other side of Jacob's bed and started pilfering through Erica's things.

There was a silver *MAC* makeup bag and it was full of MAC products. Her worn leather wallet contained $324.00, along with her driver's license and credit cards. A mini bottle of mouthwash was in the pile of stuff along with a bag of gummy worms, her cell phone, a change purse, ultrasound pictures, a book filled with baby names, soft peppermints, tooth picks, hot sauce packets, tums, coupons, a comb, brush, body spray, appointment reminders, papers from a gift registry, and a book titled *Bangles and Broken Hearts*.

"I thought I had a lot of stuff in my purse," Trudy said, as she started to put Erica's belongings back into the purse. "Hold on, let me see that baby book and that ultrasound." After looking through the book, I noticed that only girl names were highlighted. Then when I looked at the small print on the side of the ultrasound, I read the words "Baby Girl Camden." "It looks like they're having a little girl," I uttered, as I handed Trudy the baby book and the ultrasound. "Now will you give her the purse?" I asked. "Yep." Said Trudy as she left the room for a few minutes and came right back.

"What was she doing?" I asked, as soon as Trudy stepped back into the room. "She was sitting out there biting her nails. There was a young lady with her. It must've been her sister or cousin because they look alike. The both of them look like chocolate Keebler Elves." She replied. "Trudy stop it." I laughed, as the door opened. It was my youngest son Ty and not much longer after he walked in, Jr did too.

I hugged my boys and told them everything the doctor told me. They agreed that Jacob looked miserable with all of those tubes hooked up to him. We all decide that Jacob would be taken off the machines tomorrow. The beeping of the machines were driving me insane. On top of that, my nerves were a wreck because I thought that Jacob had stopped breathing twice. I was going to stay the night at the hospital, but I just couldn't.

That same evening Ty, Jr, and I contacted the rest of Jacobs family and friends and told them about the accident. We insisted that they come to see him within the next day or two because of his deteriorating condition. Most people admitted that they couldn't make it and asked for the hospital address so they could send flowers. As thoughts of planning a funeral gave me an instant headache, I thought back to my own mother's funeral and decided that I would have a viewing at the funeral home and have Jacob cremated.

At 5:16 a.m. the house phone rang. It was a nurse from the hospital. She gave me the news that Jacob had passed away. In a way, I wanted the satisfaction of pulling the plug, but I'm glad that it happened this way. I wouldn't have to deal with it on my conscience for the rest of my life. I said a prayer for him and then woke Ty and Jr up to give them the news.

***

The day after the viewing, Jacob's body was cremated. When I went to the funeral home to pick up the ashes, the little lady in the front office tried to sell me a fancy urn, but I declined. "Can I ask you a question?" "Sure dear," she responded. "Have a man ever cheated on you?" "Excuse me dear?" She asked as she looked at me like I was crazy. "Has a man ever broken your heart or maybe even crushed it?" I asked with squinted eyes. "Oh, yes ma'am. That's a terrible feeling."

"Do you think you can find a container for a low down dirty two-timing dead dog?" I asked. "Oh, he was a two-timer? Yes, dear. I have the perfect thing for Mr. Camden's ashes. Follow me." We walked down a long hallway, and she ducked inside of a closet. While peering over her shoulder, I saw her grab a box of kitty litter. After she emptied the remaining kitty litter out into a nearby litter box, I followed her back into a room that smelled like burnt coals.

As she opened a black file cabinet, I saw clear plastic bags full of charred remains. There was a tag attached to the bag that had names written on them. When I saw the tag that had Jacob's name on it, I said, "There he is." The lady picked up the bag of ashes up and asked, "Are you certain that you want Mr. Camden's ashes in that container?" As she pointed at the kitty litter box. "I sure am," I admitted, as I looked her dead in the eyes. She then slid the bag of ashes into the kitty litter box, and it fit like a glove. After she closed the cap on the box, we both giggled, and I wrote a check for the cremation services.

As I carried the box of ashes to the car, I had a bounce in my step. Before I started the car, I buckled up and buckled Jacob's ashes into the passenger seat as well. I enjoyed the smooth ride of his BMW as I took Jacob's ashes on a quick drive across town. When I reached the house that Erica and Jacob had lived in. I blew the horn twice and got the kitty litter box full of Jacob's ashes out of the passenger seat. I then popped the trunk to get a bag of gifts I had for the baby. As I stepped onto the porch with an arm full of baby goodies and the ashes of my husband, I admired the cast iron patio set.

Just as I was about to ring the doorbell, Erica opened the entry door. "What the hell do you want Kandee?" She asked, as she leaned against the frame of the door and rolled her eyes. "Oh, I just came to drop off Jacob and this stuff for the baby. Since you wanted him so bad while he was alive, I figured you'd want his ashes." I then shoved the box of ashes into her hands, and sat the bag of baby stuff down on the porch.

"I hope you have a nice life." I shouted as I headed towards my car. "You can't be serious," she screamed, as she dropped the box that held Jacob's ashes and some of the contents spilled out. "Yes, I'm dead serious. Just like Jacob," I smirked, as I buckled up and turned the ignition on. "You are one crazy bitch! Do you know that Kandee?" Erica yelled as she watched me back out of her driveway. I beeped the horn once more and yelled "I know," as I waved my hand out of the window. "Now that really felt good," I thought to myself.

17

My First Love

That next month Denise called me early one morning. After we exchanged greetings, she said, "I know that you're taking thing slow with Daniel at the moment, so I reached out and got Levi's phone number for you." I was ordering a shipment of cleaning supplies at work when she delivered the news that took me by total surprise. "What? How did you even know where to begin looking for him?" I sputtered. "I called Renee. You remember her from high school, don't you?" Denise asked. "Yeah, I remember she wrote Levi a letter back in the day, and he rejected her. If I can recall, that was right before he and I started dating." "Yes, that's her. The year after you moved, Levi and Renee started dating. They actually dated until he left to go to college." She added.

I didn't feel like ordering any more cleaning supplies while I listened to Denise. I only sat and stared at the wall while everything sank in. I learned that Levi was a high school art teacher and lived a few hours away from me here in Georgia. Even though I hadn't thought about Levi in a few weeks, I felt like I was in love with him all over again. Thoughts of marrying him and living happily ever after engulfed my mind until Denise said, "He's engaged to be married, but he still wanted me to give you his phone number." "Engaged? Is he engaged to Renee" I asked, full of jealousy. "No, he's engaged to some elementary school teacher. I looked her up, but she wasn't on Faceplace." "I'll take his number. I guess it will be okay considering that he's not officially married yet." I exclaimed, as I wrote down the number and put it in the drawer on my desk.

For the remainder of the day, I thought of Levi and couldn't wait to call him. I wondered how I would feel when I heard his voice for the first time in almost 20 years. When the time finally came to shut the kitchen down, I was beyond excited. I knew that within the hour, I would be on the phone with Levi. As I cleaned, I remembered the picture that Levi had drawn of me. I wondered what happened to it and decided that I would look for it as soon as I got home.

After I let everyone out of the restaurant, locked the door after them. Then I hurried into my office and pulled the desk drawer open. Just as I picked up my work phone to dial Levi's number, my cell phone rang. It was Daniel. I was torn, and I didn't know what to do. I knew that if I answered Daniel's call, he would probably want to talk to me until I got home. Even though I knew that it was wrong, I disregarded Daniel's call and let my cell phone ring until it went to voice mail.

While Daniel was more than likely leaving me a very nice message, I punched in Levi's number like I was calling 911 and my life depended on it. "Hello," a voice answered. "Hello is this Levi?" "Yes," he answered. "Levi, this is Kandee." "My God. It's so good to hear your voice baby. I've missed you so much." He confessed. "I've missed you too. I can't believe that I'm talking to you right now. Hearing your voice has made my day." I beamed. We talked for almost two hours, and Levi confirmed that he was engaged to be married next month.

I didn't know how I felt about Levi having a fiancée. I was a little bothered by it, but if Levi loved me like he used to. I figured he'd think about calling the wedding off to live happily ever after with me. When I found out that Levi didn't have any kids, I told him about my two boys. He was shocked to find out that I had two kids while I was in high school. I told him that I was shocked too. After we laughed, he asked me if he could keep my number and call me sometimes. Of course I didn't mind, so I told him that would be fine.

After talking to Levi that day, he called me every weekday on his thirty-minute commute to and from work. I felt excited all over again as we reminisced about our old childhood memories. Besides talking about the past, Levi caught me up with everything he'd been doing over the years. When he suggested that we meet up the following week, I eagerly agreed.

That same week we set a date to meet in a town that was an hour away from the both of us. We planned to have lunch at this place that claimed to have the best BBQ in the state of Georgia. I was so excited that I neglected most of Daniel's calls. The night before Levi and I were due to meet, Daniel suggested that I spend the night with him, but I politely declined. I told Daniel that I needed to go over some important paperwork regarding Jacob's business, and he understood. After I lied to him, I felt pretty bad, and I tossed and turned all night.

As soon as the sun made its appearance the next morning, I woke up and logged onto my Faceplace account. After looking around on the site for a while, it was time for me to get ready for my meeting with Levi. I showered, put on a pair of stretch jeans and a cream colored blouse. I curled my hair and added a little eye makeup before I hit the road. On the way to see Levi, I wondered how he would look. Since he didn't have a Faceplace account, I wasn't able to get that sneak peek, and I was a ball of nervous energy.

When I started seeing signs for the restaurant on the highway, I had a terrible urge to bite my nails. As I got off on the exit, my cell phone rang. It was Levi; he called to tell me that he was already at the restaurant and was waiting for me in the parking lot. I talked to him until I parked. I checked my face and applied some gloss on my lips before I got out of the car. Then I nervously looked around the crowded parking lot for his car.

My heart did a back flip when I saw him walking towards me. He still looked the same. He looked more like his dad with his facial hair. I couldn't believe that I was about to wrap my arms around my first love. "Damn, Kandee. You look great." He said, as he grabbed me and squeezed me tight. "You look just like your dad. It's so good to see you and finally wrap my arms around you." I excitedly responded.

After we hugged and looked each other over for a few minutes, we got in the long line at the restaurant. As packed as this place was, they must've had the best BBQ. While we waited, we talked and looked into each other's eyes. As the waitress interrupted us and showed us to a booth in the corner, I realized that I wasn't hungry anymore because I was full off of love.

Not too long after we ordered our meal, the conversation took a turn. Somehow we started talking about what we used to do whenever we were alone at his house, back in the day. "You know Levi, I had no clue what I was doing back then. All I knew is that I wanted to be close to you." I confessed as I sipped on my sweet tea. "Are you serious?" He asked. "Yeah," I replied with a smile. "Well, you always kept a smile on my face. I could never seem to get enough of you." Levi confessed as he continued to talk, "Hey, you think we could get out of here and spend some quiet time together? We don't have to do anything sexual; I only want to hold you, like I did the last time we were together."

My mama didn't raise a fool. I knew good and damn well what Levi had up his sleeve. I'm just glad that he mentioned the idea first because I was tempted to ask him as soon as he wrapped his arms around me outside. "Yes, I think I'd like that very much," I admitted, as Levi flagged the waitress down and asked for the check.

As soon as he mentioned the hotel room, I knew what was up. Levi and I were both grown now and knew what we were about to get ourselves into. I didn't feel bad about being here with him since neither one of us were married. However, I did think about Daniel for a brief second while I waited for the waitress to bring the check.

After he paid for our lunch, we both got into Levi's black Acura and headed down the road to a motel. As we pulled into the parking lot, I remembered that I'd passed this place on my way into town. When Levi parked, he turned the engine off and said, "I'll be right back." He then hopped out of the car to go inside and pay for the room. I stayed in the car until he came back with the key. As he walked back, I noticed that he still had the boyish smile that I fell in love with years ago.

The way he smiled made me think of how he used to smile at me on the school bus. When he opened his car door, he said "The room is upstairs. Are you ready?" "Yes," I answered anxiously, as I opened my door and grabbed my purse. As we walked up the stairs, we made small talk until we entered the room.

The room smelled like stale cigarette smoke, but it looked clean. After I coughed, I reached into my purse and sprayed some of my body spray around the room. Now it smelled like burnt flowers, but that was ok because I was with Levi. As soon as I put my purse down on the small table by the window, Levi moved in close and kissed me.

As we kissed, I felt like Laura Ingalls running through that field of flowers on the show *The Little House on the Prairie*. I didn't know if I was going or coming because I hadn't kissed his lips in so long. They tasted sweeter than cotton candy, and I devoured them as his hands caressed my body. While things started to heat up, the natural high that I was enjoying came to a screeching halt when Levi unfastened my blouse.

"Hold on Levi," I said, as I backed away from him. "What's wrong?" "I'm not the same girl that you used to make love to. I've changed, well what I mean is that my body has changed." I stressed. "Kandee, your body, was beautiful then, and I can appreciate the curves you have. Can't you tell?" He asked as he looked down at his erection. "Now get your ass over here. We've got some catching up to do."

I did as he insisted, and pressed my body against him. While he undressed me, his lips touched each and every part of my body. As we got comfortable on the bed, I stopped worrying about my stretch marks and enjoyed the overdue make-out session that we were having. I didn't know if I was on him or if he was on me. All I knew is that we were all over one another.

After we were both in our birthday suits, we explored each other's bodies, and I saw that Levi had changed too. He had grown in all the right places, and I couldn't wait to feel him inside of me. As we pleased each other orally, we both released moans and groans like the people from

Aunt Joyce's porn video. I guess we made so much noise because we always had to be quiet when we were younger.

Today we were going to get it all out. We didn't have anything to hide from. All we had was time and a comfy mattress. As each second passed, I became hotter and hotter. When he finally entered my wetness, I came undone quickly. As he delivered each spine-tingling thrust, my toes curled until his speed slowed down and he collapsed onto the bed beside me.

We both looked at each other and busted out laughing. "You make just as much noise as I do" I said as I twisted my fingers around in a few of his curls. "That's because you put it on me so good," he responded. After laying in silence for a few more moments, I said, "Well, I'm going to take a quick shower, if you don't mind." "Wait, Kandee. There's something that I need to get off of my chest. I'm still in love with you. Do you still love me?" He asked as he took a deep breath.

"Yes Levi, I love you, and I'm still in love with you. After all of these years, I've held a special place in my heart for you. Even though I was married, I have to admit that I've thought of you making love to me instead of my husband." I confessed. "I've thought of you and wondered where on earth you could be. When I found out that we only lived two hours away from one another, I had to see you." He said. I blushed as he took his hand and tucked my hair behind my ear.

"Do you think we'll be able to have a relationship again?" I asked. "I hope so after I get married next month. I should be able to see you at least once a month without getting caught up." He said as he tried to kiss me on my cheek. When I got up, he looked confused and said, "What's the matter. Did I say something wrong?" No, I'm going to take my shower, I should be getting back soon. After I gathered all of my belongings, I went into the bathroom and started the shower.

I don't know why I thought Levi would leave his fiancée for me, but I was shocked as hell after he busted my bubble. As I thought about confronting him about being a womanizer, I decided that there was no use. I wasn't going to play second fiddle to anyone. After all, I had been through with Jacob, I knew that being Levi's side piece was out of the question.

When I overheard him on the phone talking to someone, I turned the shower off and pressed my ear against the bathroom door. "I'm going to be home late tonight, I have to get some grades entered into the system, progress reports are scheduled to come out tomorrow. Okay, I love you too."

As I started to get dressed, I had a change of plans. With my body still damp from the shower, I wrapped a towel around my body and opened the bathroom door. Once Levi saw me standing there, he flipped his cell phone shut and looked at me. "That shower made me horny. Do you want to give it another go?" I asked as I dropped the towel. The look on Levi's face said it all. He was all over me like white on rice. He licked me from my head to my toes and then worked me over real good before he tapped out.

"I'm going to jump in the shower before I take you back to your car. Is that okay?" He asked as he sat up in bed. "Oh yeah, that's fine," I answered. After he shut the door to the bathroom, I grabbed the remote and tried to find something to watch on television. When I heard the shower come on, Levi's phone buzzed, and it got my attention. I wondered if it was his fiancée texting him. When my curiosity got the best of me, I flipped open his phone and read the text message "I hope we're still on for tomorrow night." That message was from someone named Diane.

As I dug a little deeper, I found pictures and more messages from three more women. I kept reading through Levi's messages until I heard him turn the shower off. Then I put the phone back where it was and pretended like I was watching television. After Levi put his clothes back on, we hugged and kissed for a few minutes, then we were out the door.

On the drive back home, I called Daniel and ignored Levi's calls as he beeped in several times. After reading the messages on his phone, I knew that he was just like Jacob. I didn't know how much longer I would be conversating with him on the phone. I felt some type of way, knowing that Levi was engaged to be married and juggling so many women. This was a total turn off, and I wished that I wouldn't have met with him today.

***

Over the next couple of days, I answered Levi's calls, but I didn't talk to him long. I found myself making up excuses to get off of the phone with him, and I think that he was picking up on it. One day out of the blue he asked me if I still had the drawing that he drew of me. I thought about the picture that made me feel so special back in the day and couldn't remember what happened to it. The last time I saw it, I had just had Jr and took it down off of the wall to hang some of his baby pictures. It was probably at dad's house, stuffed into one of the boxes in the attic I admitted.

"I still remember how pretty you looked when I saw you at school that day. I couldn't take my eyes off of you." He said as he reminisced. "Oh, I loved my braids. I may see if Trudy can do my hair this week." I added. After he cleared his throat and said, "Kandee, I'd like to see you again. With or without the braids." "Levi, shouldn't you be focusing your attention on your soon to be wife? I don't think it would be a good idea to tell you the truth."

"Now why would you say a thing like that?" He asked, without hesitation. "Levi, I'm going to tell you something, and I don't want you to be mad at me." "I'd never be mad at you. Tell me what's on your mind," he replied. "The other day when we were at the hotel, I looked through your text messages when you were in the shower. I saw all of the other women that you've been calling and texting. It's like you don't have any shame in your game and you..." That's all I got out before he interrupted me. "Really Kandee? Why are you so worried about my fiancée? I love you far more than I'll ever love her." He admitted, with a growl. I'd never heard him sound so aggressive; I was glad that we were on the phone and not face to face. "Well if you love me more than her, why are you marrying her instead of me then?" There was a brief moment of silence before he responded, "Kandee, I can't answer that question because I don't know the answer to it." "I can respect that, but I don't understand why you're going to marry a woman you don't really love. Are you marrying her because she's a pushover?" "I've got to go Kandee. I'll talk to you tomorrow." He said as he hung up.

That was the last conversation that I ever had with Levi. He never called me back after the conversation we had about him being a womanizer. A few days later I received a last minute invitation to his wedding. I couldn't believe that he had the nerve to invite me. I put the invitation on the counter with my pile of junk mail.

Later that night I called Trudy and caught her up with the whole Levi situation. As we talked, I logged onto my Faceplace account. While I scrolled down my timeline, I wondered if Erica had the baby yet, as I clicked onto her profile. The first picture that popped up was a beautiful baby girl that had a head full of hair. She was wrapped in a pink blanket, and Erica was holding her. The caption under the picture read "Tori Kandee Camden, 7 lbs. 10 oz." I almost spit my drink out when I saw that the baby's middle name was the same as my first name.

As I wondered why Erica gave her baby my name, I continued to look through the pictures. When I noticed that baby, Tori was dressed in one of the outfits that I had purchased for her. I wasn't sure if Erica was trying to be petty or if she was trying to send me some kind of signal without contacting me. Whatever the case, I finished my glass of wine and clicked the like button under every last one of the pictures with the baby on them. Then I logged off of Faceplace, took a shower, and called Daniel so we could have phone sex.

18

Moving On: Next month

I hadn't talked to Levi, and I had no plans of calling him. I was attached to Daniel now, and I couldn't let him go. I would be a fool to get involved with a soon to be married man and let him have his cake and eat it too. I couldn't even believe that Levi wanted me to be his part-time lover. What kind of pathetic sap did he think I was? I loved him, but it was time to let what he and I used to have go.

My Life was finally going well, and I wasn't going to mess it up by running after my high school crush. The hold that Levi had on me wasn't as strong as it used to be. I looked at him differently now, and I even wished that we wouldn't have had sex. I mean there was nothing that I could do to change the fact that Levi and I had made love, so I just accepted the fact and tried not to think about it. There was no use in dwelling in the past. It happened, and that was that.

A week after Levi and I had gotten busy in the hotel, I officially became Daniel's lady, and he asked me to move in with him. I started to say no, but I was falling in love with him and wanted to take a chance on love. The same week I told Ty and Jr about deciding to sell the house and moving in with Daniel. They thought that it was a great idea. They didn't like that I lived alone and said that they felt better knowing that I would be with Daniel.

After I had got the approval from my boys, I talked to a real estate agent and put my house on the market. It only took two weeks for the house to sell and I received the full asking price. I moved in with Daniel and bought him a new moving truck. He was so surprised that he made me dinner, and we ate in the back of it one night. I upgraded to a 2010 Volvo and put an ad in the paper to sell Jacob's BMW. I didn't need two cars. I figured that I could invest the money I made in my very own restaurant one day.

***

The day before Levi's wedding, I went to my old house and checked the mail one last time. As I pulled halfway up in the driveway and put my car in park, I looked at the house long and hard. As Groove Theory's, *Get Up* played in the background, I thought about how the boys and I decorated for Halloween, Christmas, and had Easter egg hunts in the backyard. While we did all of those things, Jacob wasn't anywhere around.

It was almost like I raised Ty and Jr all by myself. Jacob was always gone on business trips or doing something with the military guys. That's why Ty and Jr love me so much. I know they loved Jacob, but they were truly mama's boys. If they had to choose between the two of us, I would be their pick. No doubt about it.

As I sat there, I got a bit sentimental. I stared at the house until my cell phone started ringing. When I dug my phone out of the bottom of my purse, I saw Levi's unsaved number lighting up on the screen. I wondered what he wanted. I already told him that I didn't want to be a part of his little game. I wanted to answer his call, but with Levi getting married tomorrow. I knew that it wouldn't be such a great idea.

After I had taken a deep breath, I put the ringing phone in the cup holder and got out of the car. I wasn't going to go into the house, but I still had the keys, and the new owners didn't change the locks yet. I decided that I would go in one last time. Up the driveway I walked, when I made it onto the porch, I opened the screen door and pressed my face against the glass in the entry door. I didn't see anyone, so I unlocked the door and let myself in. Considering that the place I'd just walked into had been my home for over 15 years, I felt out of place. There was no warmth anywhere, and my footsteps echoed as walked through the newly abandoned house.

I made my way up the stairs and did one final check. I looked inside of the closets, under the sinks in the bathrooms, and kitchen and there wasn't anything left. Daniel, Jr, Ty, and I did an excellent job moving our things out. I looked around one last time before I locked the entry door and walked towards the mailbox. I waved to one of my former neighbors, as I opened the latch on the shiny black mailbox. There were two envelopes inside. After pulling both pieces of mail out, I saw that the bigger envelope didn't have a return address on it. Even though I was curious about the big envelope, I read the heading on the small envelope instead. I knew it was something from the insurance company because of the sender's address.

This had to be one of the checks from the insurance policies that I had on Jacob. With fast hands, I tore open the envelope. After pulling out the folded papers that were inside, I saw that one of the two papers had a check attached to it. I thought my eyes were deceiving me, but the amount of the check was for 25,000 dollars. I was so happy that I felt like screaming. But I only did a little dance and stuffed the check down into my bra.

With all the excitement about the check, I forgot about the stiff envelope and ran to my car. I had to put this check in the bank before it closed. Before I backed out if the driveway, I called Trudy and told her about the check. She was just as excited as I was about the check and asked to borrow five dollars. I had laughed at her joke before she asked, "How do you feel about Levi getting married tomorrow?" "I don't know. I can't believe that he wants me to come to his wedding." I replied as I pulled into the parking lot at the bank.

"I don't know what's up with him; he knows that he still wants you, but he's still getting married," Trudy said. "I'm not going to go. I think he wants me to make a scene like Dewayne Wane did at Whitley's wedding on *A Different World*," I giggled. After Trudy had burst out laughing, she said, "I think that what you and Daniel have going on will work out. You two are so much alike that it's scary. The two of you like the same music, love to cook, and love to entertain. I hope you invite me over there the next time all of Daniel's friends come over. I might be able to find a new lover." "He has some cute friends. I'll definitely let you know the next time they come over."

After I deposited the insurance check into my bank account. I went to the grocery store and picked up a few items; then I made my way home. As soon as I grabbed my purse out of the passenger seat, I saw the big stiff envelope. I had totally forgotten about it. When I picked it up, my heart rate increased. I was bugging out, but after the thought of some important legal documents pertaining to Jacob's estate; I quickly and carefully opened the envelope.

When I pulled out the card stock, I was left speechless. There was a perfect drawing of me. Back when I was in high school. I had the beautiful braids that Trudy had spent all afternoon doing on the front porch. This was the same drawing that Levi had drawn for me almost 20 years ago. Now I knew who and where the envelope came from. I only smiled and looked at the picture. The memories from my childhood were right in front of me, all over again.

The realness of the picture was unbelievable. I noticed how my brown eyes sparkled. My lips were plump and shaded with the prettiest shade of pastel pink. Levi even drew my baby hairs and the necklace that he had given me for Christmas. After seeing this picture, I wanted to talk to Levi more than ever, but I resisted the urge.

After I had gone inside I put my new picture in a box with Levi's letters and his pillowcase. Then I went back outside to get the groceries from out of the car. While I started dinner, I called Trudy and told her about the drawing. Of course she wanted to see it, so I took a picture of it with my phone and sent it to her. When the message finally made it through, she hollered, "Kandee, this looks just like you. I feel as if I'm looking at you through my young eyes all over again. Man, those were the days."

"Yes, those were the days, if I could turn back the hands of time and get the old Levi back. I would." I said.

"It's too bad he's gone. Levi's someone else now, and he's about to be married tomorrow. I don't think I should keep this picture, the letters, or pillowcase any longer." I uttered, as I put a pot of veggies on the stove. "Well, do you want me to keep them at my house?" Trudy asked. "No, that's not going to do it. It's time for this box to go. I'm going to call you back in bit." I responded as I retrieved the box of letters out of a large cardboard box in the corner of the living room. "Okay. Don't forget about me. You know how you get when Daniel comes home." Trudy joked as she hung up.

Before I could even think about what I was doing, I was already in Daniel's office. I plugged the cord to his shredder into the socket. While I asked myself if I really wanted to do this, my eyes got misty. I unfolded the letters one by one and fed them into the shredder. When there was nothing left but the pillowcase, I emptied the trash into the pillowcase and shoved the old shoe box in it as well. On my way back to the kitchen, I grabbed the beautiful picture of myself off of the counter and ripped it up.

I wiped the tears off of my cheeks with the collar of my shirt. Then I put the confetti-size pieces of the picture into the pillowcase with the rest of my shredded memories from Levi. After I had tied the pillowcase up, I opened the lid on the trash can and dropped the pillowcase in with the egg shells and onion peelings. Then I removed the entire trash bag from the can and pulled the strings so that I could tie them into a knot.

On my way out the back door, I heard Daniel's moving truck pulling into the driveway. As I walked a little faster, I said "Hey baby, I was just taking out the trash. How was your day?" "It was good, but the last thing I expected to see when I came home was you taking out a bag of nasty trash," he replied as I tossed the bag of memories from my past into the bin. "You know that's my job. I don't want to see you taking out the garbage again. You're too pretty to be doing that." He added as he walked towards me. "Well, that was some old stuff that I should've thrown away ages ago. Do you forgive me?" I asked, with a flirtatious smile. "If you give me a kiss, I'm sure that I could forgive you," he replied, as he winked his eye at me.

We met each other halfway on the lawn, I leaned into his arms and tilted my head back. As he bent down to kiss me, I realized that butterflies were dancing in the pit of my stomach. Something about that feeling made me feel brand new all over again. When our lips met and our tongues mingled, I became somewhat weak in the knees. At that exact moment, the hold that Levi had on me vanished and my crush no longer existed. I knew without a doubt that Daniel was my soul mate, and I couldn't wait to make sweet love to him tonight.